# SAVING KYLA

## BROTHERHOOD PROTECTORS YELLOWSTONE
### BOOK #1

## ELLE JAMES

TWISTED PAGE INC

# SAVING KYLA

## BROTHERHOOD PROTECTORS
## YELLOWSTONE BOOK #1

*New York Times & USA Today*
Bestselling Author

**ELLE JAMES**

*Dedicated to Bandit and Charli, my two Yorkies.*
*I love them dearly.*
*Elle James*

# AUTHOR'S NOTE

Enjoy other military books by Elle James

**Brotherhood Protectors Yellowstone**
**Brotherhood Protectors Yellowstone**
Saving Kyla (#1)
Saving Chelsea (#2)
Saving Amanda (#3)
Saving Liliana (#4)
Saving Breely (#5)
Saving Savvie (#6)
Saving Jenna (#7)

Visit ellejames.com for titles and release dates
For hot cowboys, visit her alter ego Myla Jackson at
mylajackson.com
and join Elle James's Newsletter at
https://ellejames.com/contact/

# CHAPTER 1

KYLA RUSSELL WAS DONE with killing.

Especially when her target didn't deserve to die.

Camouflaged as an Afghan male in a long white thobe, the ankle-length white shirt Afghan men wore, she stood on a street in Kandahar, Afghanistan, a pistol with a silencer attached strapped to her thigh. Beneath the thobe, she wore dark jeans and a dark shirt for night movement.

She'd pulled her long, black hair up and wrapped it in a dark turban like the ones worn by men in the city. To complete her disguise, she'd applied a fake beard, bushy eyebrows and dark makeup to make her appear more masculine and able to walk freely around the city of over six hundred thousand people.

Kyla had spent the better part of the day before studying her target, both through the windows of his home and by tailing him as he'd left for work and returned. What about this man made him toxic? Why had her government deemed him dangerous to the world?

She made it a priority to research her assignments, to find out about the persons she was assigned to eliminate. Prior to accepting her current mission, she'd reviewed the dossier her handler had given her for Abdul Naser Ahmadi and had done her own background check on the man via her connections on the internet and the Dark Web.

The dossier had listed Ahmadi as an arms trafficker, supplying American weapons to the Taliban. Nothing in Kyla's own research indicated the same. In fact, Ahmadi was like a black hole of information. All she could find was that he lived with his wife in Kandahar and worked at a local university as a professor of language and literature.

Kyla had no qualms about ridding the world of pedophiles or people who tortured and killed others for their race or religious beliefs. She'd taken out cult leaders who'd planned terrorist activities in the United States and some who were killers in foreign countries.

Some of her targets had been dirty politicians, selling secrets to US enemies, placing her country's military in jeopardy. Those targets, she'd taken out with no problem and no regrets. The world was a better place without them.

Kyla took pride in never completing a mission without first understanding the target and the necessity of taking him out.

Ahmadi was not raising any red flags. Still, she planned to observe the man for a couple of days in case she was wrong.

Standing on a street corner, her back to the wall of a building, she casually observed Ahmadi at a local tea shop where he sat with another man. Maybe this was the reason for the hit—this meeting with Ahmadi's guest.

Using her cellphone, Kyla snapped a picture of the man and sent it to her contact on the Dark Web, who had access to facial recognition software.

Within minutes she was surprised to receive a response.

Jalal Malik CIA.

Kyla frowned at the message. *CIA? What the hell?*

Kyla sent the picture of Malik and Ahmadi along with a message to an old friend she'd known from her days in the CIA. A man who had access to more than he should.

Jalal Malik CIA…Legit? Clean?

Her contact responded several minutes later:

Born in the US to first-generation Afghans who escaped Afghanistan and Taliban rule thirty years before and earned their US citizenship. Malik speaks fluent Pashto and joined the CIA to give back to the country that saved his parents. Now working to uncover a mole in the US government, who is feeding information and arms to the Taliban. Ahmadi is his trusted informant.

With Ahmadi in her sights, Kyla could have

picked him off any time that day and disappeared. However, she couldn't pull the trigger, not when her gut told her something was off. Ahmadi wasn't dangerous to the US. In fact, his willingness to help the US find the traitor within made him an asset and put him in danger of Taliban retaliation. Why had he been targeted for extermination?

She'd followed him home to ask him that question. By the time he'd returned to his home, darkness had settled over Kandahar.

Kyla ducked into the shadows of the wall surrounding Ahmadi's home, where she stripped out of the white thobe and trousers and tucked them behind a stack of stones. Then she pulled herself up and over the wall, dropped down into Ahmadi's yard and watched for her chance to corner the target.

That chance presented itself within the hour.

Ahmadi's wife had gone to the bedroom. Ahmadi stepped out his back door onto the hardpacked dirt within the stone wall to smoke a cigarette.

Kyla slipped up behind him, clamped her hand over his mouth and pressed a pistol with the silencer attachment to his temple. She lowered her voice and spoke in Pashto, "Tell me why my government wants you dead."

He stood still, making no attempt to fight back. "Who is your government?"

She nudged his temple with the pistol. "The same government who sent your guest at tea."

He nodded and switched to English. "Perhaps we

are getting too close to the truth," he said in a whisper.

Kyla released the man and stepped back, her weapon trained on Ahmadi's chest as he turned to face her, his hands raised.

"I am not your enemy," he said.

"Then why would my government send me to kill you?" she asked.

He shook his head. "For the same reason I had tea with another citizen of your country. One of your own is playing for the other side and has sent you to do his dirty work."

"What do you know that would make someone put a hit out on you?" she asked.

"If you will not kill me, I will tell you what I told my guest at tea." Ahmadi's eyes narrowed as he awaited her response.

Kyla lowered her weapon. She could still kill him if he made a move to hurt her.

Ahmadi drew in a deep breath and let it out slowly before speaking again. "I received the name of the man who has been coordinating shipments to the Taliban. He goes by...Abaddon."

"Abaddon?"

The man nodded. "The meaning of the name is destruction."

At that moment, Ahmadi's wife called out in Pashto, "Are you expecting a delivery? A van just arrived in front of our gate."

Ahmadi glanced toward the house.

A knot of foreboding formed in Kyla's gut. "Call your wife to you."

Ahmadi frowned. "Why?"

"Just do it. Now." Kyla turned and slipped between the wall and the house.

Behind her, Ahmadi called to his wife.

Through the windows, Kyla could see Ahmadi's wife moving toward the back of the house.

Kyla slowed at the front corner and peered through the wrought iron gate at a dark van parked on the street. A door opened, and a man dressed in dark clothes and a ski mask dropped down.

If the mask wasn't enough to make her blood run cold, the mini machine gun he carried did the trick.

Kyla's pulse slammed through her veins. She spun and raced to the back of the house, where Ahmadi and his wife stood together.

Kyla glanced at the wall she'd scaled easily. Ahmadi and his wife would not go over it as quickly, dressed as they were in long robes.

In Pashto, she said, "Over the wall. Hurry." She bent and cupped her hands.

Ahmadi urged his wife to go first.

She hung back.

"Go," Kyla urged. "Or we all die."

The woman stepped into Kyla's palms. With her husband pushing from behind, she landed on her stomach and swung her leg over the top of the stone wall. She dropped to the other side.

Kyla held her hands for Ahmadi.

"No, you go first," Ahmadi said.

"No time to argue," she remained bent over.

Ahmadi stepped into her hands.

Kyla straightened.

Ahmadi pulled himself up to the top of the wall and reached down to give her a hand up.

She shook her head. "Go!"

He slipped over the wall and dropped to the ground on the other side.

Doors slammed open inside the house as the man in the black ski mask worked his way through the rooms. It wouldn't take him long. The house wasn't that big.

Kyla got a short, running start, scaled the wall and slung her leg over.

As she slipped over the top, she glanced back. The man in the black ski mask had just reached the back door and flung it open. Before he could see her, she dropped to the other side.

Her turban caught on a crack in the wall. Unable to stop and free it, she let it go, the ponytail she'd wound around her head shaking loose. She didn't have time to retrieve her thobe. It didn't matter. Without the turban, the disguise was useless. All she could do was run. She raced after Ahmadi and his wife.

They ran for several city blocks. The couple wouldn't be able to keep up the pace for long.

Kyla glanced over her shoulder. The man in black rounded a corner and sprinted toward them.

"Turn left," Kyla yelled to the couple. They did, and Kyla followed. "Keep going and find a safe place to hide. I'll take care of him." She stopped running and waited for the assassin to catch up.

Ahmadi and his wife turned another corner, zigzagging through the streets.

Kyla waited, her gun poised and ready. When the man didn't burst around the corner as she expected, she eased her head around.

Several yards away, the man was climbing into the van's passenger side. Once he was in, the van leaped forward, headed for her corner.

Kyla aimed at the driver's windshield and fired.

Her bullet pierced the window.

The van swerved and then straightened, coming straight for her position on the corner.

She fired again.

This time the van swerved and slid sideways into a building.

The man in the ski mask jumped out of the passenger side and, using the door for cover, aimed his rifle at Kyla.

Knowing her pistol didn't have the range or accuracy of the shooter's rifle, she backed away from the corner and ran. She had to get to a better position to defend herself or get the hell away.

She was halfway to the next corner when tires squealed behind her.

A glance over her shoulder confirmed...the van was back in action and barreling toward her.

In front of her, headlights flashed as a small sedan turned onto the street. A man leaned out of the passenger window with a rifle and fired at her.

*Fuck.*

The bullets hit the pavement beside her. Kyla turned right onto the street nearest her and ducked behind the first home she came to. She circled the house, leaping over piles of stones and brick, and hid in the shadows near the rear of the home as the sedan turned onto the street. The van was slowing as it approached the corner.

As the van turned, Kyla aimed at the front tire of the van and popped off a round. The tire blew and sent the van veering toward the front of the house behind which she hid and crashed into the front entrance.

Kyla didn't wait for the driver to recover. She backtracked and ran back in the direction from which she'd come, zigzagging between houses, hugging the shadows as she went. Several times, she was certain she glimpsed the sedan.

She hoped Ahmadi and his wife had made good their escape. After she'd split from them, she was certain the attackers had been after her. They had to know she wasn't Ahmadi. Her long ponytail would have given her away.

Making her way through the darkened streets, she pulled off the fake beard and eyebrows, wincing as the glue proved stubborn. She couldn't stay in Kandahar. Not dressed as she was. The Taliban patrolled the streets day and night, looking for people breaking the newly enforced laws. She would be arrested or beaten for her lack of appropriate attire.

Not knowing exactly who the attackers were, she couldn't afford to be caught. If they were members of the elite team of assassins she was a part of, they would know they were chasing her—and they were aiming for her, specifically.

As of that moment, she no longer worked for the US government. She was now a threat to the people who'd trained and recruited her. They'd be looking for her in Kandahar. She no longer had the support to get her out of the country. If she wanted out, she'd have to find her own way.

*Double fuck.*

Kyla made her way to the edge of the city, moving quickly. She had to get out before sunrise. She couldn't trust anyone. People wouldn't be willing to help her. Not a lone female without male protection. Especially dressed as a Westerner in pants, not wearing the mandated black abaya.

As she arrived on the edge of the city, she paused in the shadows of a fuel station.

A truck pulled up, loaded with bags of onions, oranges and various other produce. From the direction it had come, it was heading out of town for an early morning delivery.

Kyla waited for the driver to fill his tank and pay the attendant.

When he finally climbed back into the cab and started his engine, Kyla made her move.

The truck pulled out from beneath the light from a single bulb hanging over the pump and slowly picked up speed on the road heading west.

Kyla glanced left and then right.

The attendant had returned to the inside of the station. No other vehicles were in sight.

She took off, sprinting after the truck, grabbed the side rail and vaulted up into the back, landing on a stack of bagged oranges. Adjusting several heavy bags, she created a hole and fit herself into the middle, out of sight of other traffic that might pass them on the road. She settled back, praying when they stopped that she could find a way out of Afghanistan and back to the States.

Once there, she'd use her nefarious contacts in the Dark Web and her former colleagues in the CIA to find out what the hell had just happened.

THE BUMPY ROAD and the sway of the old vehicle must have lulled her to sleep.

When the truck slowed and made a couple of sharp turns, Kyla's eyes blinked, and she stared up at the sun beating down on her and the buildings on either side of the truck as it maneuvered into a small village at the edge of the hills. She guessed it was making a delivery stop, which meant she needed to get out before the driver brought the truck to a complete stop.

Kyla pushed the bags of oranges out of the way and scooted toward the tailgate. As the truck turned another corner, she dropped out of the back and rolled in the dust into the shadows, coming to a stop when she bumped up against a pair of boots.

# CHAPTER 2

"Thanks, Hank. I know the sacrifice you're making to do this. I can only imagine the incredible number of hoops you jumped through to make this happen," Stone Jacob said into the mic attached to the military-grade helmet he'd purchased for himself and the other men on his team. Only the best for the Stone Security Specialists.

For all the good it had done.

Hank dipped his head. "It's a sacrifice you'd have made for my men and me."

"Maybe. Though I'm not sure I could've pulled this off without your connections."

The helicopter lifted off from a valley tucked away in the Afghanistan hills in Helmand Province.

Stone stared out the open door into the darkness. "I bet your wife had a heart attack when you told her where you were going."

Hank's lips thinned. "Sadie wasn't thrilled, but she

understood. Our citizens...our former military men didn't deserve to be left behind when the US pulled out of Afghanistan."

Stone nodded, his hands curling into fists. "If I hadn't been in the States negotiating contracts for additional weapons and missions, I would've been with them, behind Taliban lines."

Hank snorted. "What isn't behind Taliban lines now in Afghanistan?"

"Makes my stomach knot," Stone said. "All the years we fought to push the Taliban out of Afghanistan, and our government just handed it back to them."

Hank nodded. "And did a fucked-up job of pulling out and stranding our people and those who'd helped us in our fight against the Taliban."

Stone shot a glance toward Hank, his friend from long ago when they'd been on the same SEAL team. "Makes you wonder if any of our efforts and the lives we lost meant anything."

Hank didn't respond. He didn't have to. Most military men and women who'd survived deployment to Afghanistan had strong opinions about the US backing out when and how they did.

But it was done. And the fallout was still being felt months later.

Stone had tried, to no avail, to get his guys out through talks with the Taliban. But all that had accomplished was to hang targets on their backs. They'd had to retreat into the hills and hide until

Stone could figure another way to sneak them out without the Taliban's knowledge.

When he'd exhausted all diplomatic avenues, he'd reached out to the one man who might have half a chance of coming up with a plan to extract the six men who'd been stranded now, living off the land and through the grace of Afghan citizens, risking their lives to help the Americans.

Stone glanced around at the men Hank had gathered for the mission.

He knew Boomer, the six-foot-tall, black-haired, gray-eyed man to Stone's left. The SEAL had been on active duty when Stone had, assigned to another team. The SEAL community was a small one. Boomer had a stellar record and reputation.

The same went for Trevor, a couple of inches shorter than Boomer. The man kept his dark hair short and brown eyes sharp. Stone had never met Trevor, but he knew of him. Again, he'd heard nothing but good of the man and his abilities as a SEAL.

Zach Jones, another member of Hank's Brotherhood Protectors had been an Army Ranger, who'd deployed to Iraq and Afghanistan multiple times during his career. He was battle-seasoned and capable.

Across from Stone sat a black-haired man with piercing blue eyes. Hank had introduced him as Joseph Kuntz—Kujo, to his team. A former Delta

Force operative, the man was intense. Hank had a high opinion of his skills as a soldier and leader.

Bryce Coleman, former Green Beret, not long off active duty, had been snagged from the Brotherhood Protectors Colorado team. Fresh to the organization, he'd been available and eager to help.

Stone shook his head as he stared at the men willing to go into extremely hostile territory in a land-locked nation surrounded by other countries not too pleased or friendly to Americans. "How did you manage to get a Black Hawk, C-17 airplane and the crews to fly them into Afghanistan?"

Hank gave Stone a tight grin. "I called in some favors. The men flying the birds were volunteers and members of black ops teams. They know what they're getting into. It's imperative that we get to your men, get them out of the hills and back to that dirt landing strip before the Taliban finds our plane."

Stone's hand tightened around his rifle. "Thankfully, my guys still have their satellite trackers." Stone held up the hand-held tracking device. "And Bubba still has his and the satellite phone."

"How are they keeping their electronics charged?"

"Solar power," Stone said.

"Smart," Hank said. "If there's one thing there's an abundance of in Afghanistan, it's sunshine."

The pilot's voice sounded in their headsets. "Ten clicks from our coordinates."

Hank's gaze swept over each of his men. "Gird your loins, team. It's showtime."

The men double-checked their weapons, patted the additional magazines full of ammunition tucked into the pockets of their body armor vests and gave thumbs up.

With the doors wide open, Stone could see out the side of the helicopter, not so much what was in front.

From what Bubba, Benjamin Yates, had described, they had been holed up in a cave in the hills west of a small village. After studying the topography of the hills, their plan was to land close to the caves, collect their men and head back to the C-17.

The satellite phone clipped to Stone's shoulder strap rang. Stone yanked it free and pushed his helmet up so that he could press the phone to his ear. "Jacobs here."

"Abort mission!" Bubba yelled into Stone's ear. "We've got company. Have to bug out. Don't risk it. Not sure we'll make it out before we're overrun. Fuck!"

The popping sound of gunfire sounded in the receiver.

"We're close," Stone insisted.

"Don't," Bubba said. "Too many." More gunfire. "We're low on ammo. Won't last long. Have to go deeper, if we can."

"How many?" Stone demanded.

"At least a dozen, maybe more."

"A dozen or more, advancing on their location," Stone repeated for Hank.

Hank relayed the information to the pilot and held out his hand.

Stone passed the satellite phone to Hank.

"Can you hold them off for a few minutes?" Hank asked. "We're coming in. When you hear us, take cover and switch to our radio frequency."

Hank handed the phone back to Stone, his face set in tight lines. "We're not leaving without them."

Stone sent a prayer to the heavens. A bad situation was about to get worse. Thank God, Hank hadn't backed down.

The Black Hawk picked up speed and raced for the hillside where Stone's men were surrounded and running out of ammo.

Stone's heart pounded to the beat of the rotor blades. As they neared the fight, he squared his shoulders and braced himself for the task ahead.

The chopper pilot slowed the aircraft. A moment later the *brrrrpppp* of the gunner letting loose a burst from the .50 caliber mounted machine guns sounded. The door gunners poised with their machine guns pointed at the side of the hill where tracer rounds lit up the night like so many fireworks.

"Going in hot," Hank said. "Grab a line."

The team members each grabbed a line and waited for their cue. The .50 caliber machine guns ripped off another round.

"Go!" Hank shouted.

The men dropped out of the helicopter, holding tightly to the lines with their gloved hands and slid the fifty feet toward the ground. Above them, the machine guns provided cover, firing off rounds to keep the Taliban hunkered down and unable to aim at the men as they dropped to the dirt.

Once down, Stone checked his tracking device. As he suspected the dark spot on the side of the hill was the cave where the men had sought shelter while they'd waited for their ride home.

And somewhere halfway up that hill was a dozen or so Taliban fighters. Hopefully, the bullets fired from the Black Hawk had found their marks on some of the enemy. It was up to Stone, Hank and the other members of the Brotherhood Protectors to clean up the rest.

"Make it quick," Hank said into their headsets. "Our Uber driver just spotted a truck full of men headed this way to join the party. Boomer, Stone and I'll provide cover. Kujo, Zach, Trev, Cole —you're up."

The team leapfrogged up the hill, closing in on the Taliban fighters, while Stone, Boomer and Hank hung back and provided cover, firing over their heads toward the shadowy figures hugging the hill-side and the boulders littering the slope.

"We're down," Kujo's voice said into Stone's ear.

"Coming," Hank responded.

Stone, Boomer and Hank moved up the hill, hunkering as low as possible to the ground.

Ahead of them, Kujo's contingent fired into the darkness.

"One down, twelve to go," Kujo said. "Cole nailed one. We can see them moving up to the cave."

"Can't let them get there," Stone said. "My guys will be out of ammunition."

Stone and the others knew that if the Taliban got there before they could stop them, the men in the cave would be killed or taken prisoner. Then the Taliban would have a stronghold. Hank and his team wouldn't be able to lob grenades into their midst or shoot into the cave for fear of hitting one of the Americans.

"No time to play it safe," Stone said. "Let's do this." He charged past the point men's positions and fired at any shadow heading toward the mouth of the cave.

Hank ran with him and Kujo fell in on his right. The others fanned out and swept up the slope, firing their weapons.

"Bubba," Stone said into his mic, breathing hard as he pushed hard to get to his guys. "You copy?"

Static filled his ear.

He cursed.

"Bubba here," a voice crackled in the static.

"Staying down?"

"It's all we can do. All out of bullets. All we have are rocks."

"Hang tight. We're on our way," Hank said.

Bullets flew past Stone. In his peripheral vision, he saw one of Hank's men stumble and fall.

This was not what he'd wanted. Trading lives for lives? No. Stone wouldn't let it happen. He yelled as he ran up the hill, spraying fire in a sweeping motion until his magazine ran dry. Quickly ejecting the empty, he jammed a full one in its place and kept firing.

Something stung his arm. He didn't slow, didn't acknowledge the pain, just kept moving.

Ahead a man leaned out from around a boulder.

Stone dropped to a knee and fired, hitting the man square in the chest.

*Two down, ten to go, he thought to himself.* He didn't say it out loud, not when he needed to preserve his air to make it to the top of the hill.

Another man stood.

Hank fired.

The man dropped and rolled a few feet down the slope.

As best they could, they moved from boulder to boulder or bush to bush, advancing closer to the mouth of the cave. As were the Taliban fighters.

The team's sheer audacity seemed to have slowed their enemy's ascent, allowing Stone and Hank's team to gain ground. The closer they moved toward the enemy, the more dangerous it became.

It finally came down to a firefight between the two sides.

"They aren't moving," Hank whispered into their headsets. "Stay down and let them think they got us."

"We don't have much time to wait them out," Kujo said. "Not with another truckload of trouble on its way. The wind's in our favor. I'm popping smoke. We have to make a run for it."

"Okay. Go for it," Hank said. "Be ready."

Moments later, a smoke grenade sailed through the air, landing between the team and the Taliban.

Smoke billowed from the canister, filling the air. A slight breeze blew it toward the Taliban.

As the smoke blinded them, the enemy fired their weapons indiscriminately.

"Go!" Hank urged.

The men moved up the hill, staying within sight of the man next to them to keep from shooting each other.

A silhouette emerged in front of Stone, his rifle aimed at Stone's chest.

Stone fired.

The man fell, his weapon discharging as he fell to the ground. The bullet flew close past Stone's ear. Had he been an inch to his left…

*Three down. No time to spare.*

In the lead, Stone topped the rise and dove into the darkness of the cave. "Don't shoot. It's me, Stone," he said as he came up on his hands and knees.

"Hold your fire," Bubba said aloud. "He's one of us."

Hank and Kujo burst into the cave next, turned and covered while the others followed.

The last man in was Zach, the one who'd been shot. Limping, he'd still made the climb up the hill with the others.

Stone laid down his rifle and pulled the strap of the small submachine gun he'd carried with him over his head. He handed the weapon and a couple of magazines filled with bullets to the man. "Can you all get back down the hill?"

"We can now," Bubba said.

Each of the members of Hank's team had carried an extra weapon with them. They handed over pistols, submachine guns and rifles to Stone's men while Hank and Kujo fired into the night at the Taliban as a breeze carried the last of the smoke away.

"They're making a run for us," Kujo said.

"We've got this. Get ready for a big bang." Hank grabbed a grenade from a clip on his vest, pulled the pin, tossed the grenade and ducked his head.

Stone dropped to the ground and covered his ears.

A second later, an explosion rocked the ground beneath them. Dust filled the air.

"Let's move." Hank leaped to his feet and exited the cave, half-running, half-sliding down the slope, his rifle held out in front of him.

Stone stayed behind, waiting for his men to make it out. As he counted the number of men leaving the cave, he watched for any movement from the Taliban fighters.

Hank's team was first out. Stone's men ran out of the cave one by one. He counted five and then another, smaller man flew past him and out of the cave. He slipped and landed on his ass, sliding down the hill like he was on a child's playground.

*Six men. That isn't right.*

Stone didn't have time to ponder the extra body.

A man leaped out from behind a large rock and aimed at Hank and his team.

Stone sighted in and pulled the trigger.

The first shot hit the man in the arm, forcing him to drop his weapon.

Almost caught up with Hank, Bubba finished the Taliban guy off with a well-placed shot to the chest. He hadn't even slowed his descent. The man was a skilled marksman, no matter the conditions.

When the last man beside himself was halfway down the hill, Stone started down.

Shots were fired, but he was moving so fast now, skidding, slipping and sliding his way downward, he didn't try to fire back. His goal was to get the hell out of there.

Below him, he saw the headlights of a truck approaching from the east. It was getting close. They'd be hard-pressed to get to their pickup point in time for the helicopter to land and take them out.

"Go! Go! Go!" he called out. His foot hit a rock, and he pitched forward, tumbling, somersaulting and rolling the rest of the way to the bottom. He held onto his rifle all the way down, his arms, legs and body taking the brunt of the fall. When he finally came to a stop, he pushed to his feet, thankful no bones were broken. Every inch of his body would be bruised, but he could still move.

Ahead of him, Zach was limping toward their extraction point.

Hank and Kujo were covering for them as the men ran for the open space where the helicopter would land to pick them up.

Stone ran for Zach, looped his rifle strap over his shoulder and hooked his arm around Zach's waist. Together, they ran, limping and hobbling.

When Zach stumbled, Stone went down with him.

Bubba appeared beside them, threw Zach over his shoulder and took off.

Stone brought his weapon to the ready and turned back to see Hank and Kujo heading his way.

The thunder of rotor blades heralded the Black Hawk's approach.

Gunfire sounded from the hillside.

Stone returned fire, allowing Hank and Kujo to race past him.

A blast from the helicopter's guns gave Stone his opportunity to make a run for it. Hank and Kujo helped the others board before they climbed on.

Stone had just reached them when the helicopter lifted off the ground. "Everybody on board?" he yelled.

"Yes! Jump!" Hank shouted and leaned down, holding out his hand.

Stone ran and leaped into the air, extending his arms.

Hank grabbed one hand, Kujo caught the other and they pulled him into the aircraft.

Stone landed on his belly on the metal floor of the chopper.

The door gunner fired his Dillon Minigun at the hillside as the Black Hawk rose into the air.

Below, the truck had just arrived at the base of the hill. The men in the back leaped out and fired into the air.

"Shit," Hank said. "One of them has an RPG!"

The pilot swung the Black Hawk around and unleashed a missile on the truck at the same time the RPG went off.

"Incoming!" Stone shouted.

The RPG's missile blasted toward them.

If ever there was a time when Stone saw his life pass before his eyes, it was then.

As soon as he'd fired the missile at the truck, the pilot spun the tail around. The RPG rocket missed the Black Hawk and crashed into a hill nearby, rocking the aircraft.

Seated on the metal floor, Stone slid toward the open door. Boomer grabbed his arm before he could fall out.

The helicopter righted itself and rose high into the air, out of range of the rifle fire.

Boomer dragged Stone up onto the bench beside him.

"Thanks." Stone settled in for the ride back to the plane. As the adrenaline rush subsided, every bruise and cut made itself known across his body.

He looked around at the familiar if dirty faces of the men he'd recruited and trained to provide security for different companies operating in Afghanistan.

Bubba leaned forward from where he sat on the other side of Boomer and held out his hand. "We owe you. Thanks."

"You don't owe me a thing. If anything, I owe you an apology for not getting you out sooner." Stone gripped Bubba's hand. "And don't thank me. Thank Hank." He tipped his head toward Hank. "And don't thank either of us until we're on the plane out of here," Hank muttered.

"You got us out of that damned cave." Carter Manning grasped Stone's hand as soon as Bubba released it.

"Carter," Stone said. "Good to see your ugly face."

The man grinned. "Back atcha."

Stone looked to Carter's left. "Dax? Is that you under all that dirt?"

"Damn right, it is." Daxton Young held up a hand in greeting, too far over to shake Stone's hand. His blond hair was a dark, dirty brown, but those blue eyes were hard to miss. "I'd give my left nut for a shower and a steak."

"Keep your nuts," Stone said. "When we get back to the states, I'll get you that steak. You're on your own for the shower." Stone grinned. "Glad you made it."

Dax sighed. "Me, too."

Hunter waved from the far side of Dax. "Thanks, Stone. You don't look so pretty yourself."

Stone gave the man a chin lift. "I decided a little gymnastics were in order to get down that hill a bit faster." He frowned and glanced around. "Where's Moe?"

Morris Cleveland leaned around Hunter's big frame. "Yo, Stone. I'm here."

Kujo sat on the floor of the helicopter, working on Zach's leg.

"Is he going to be okay?" Stone asked Hank.

Hank nodded. "Should be. He didn't lose too much blood, and Kujo's wrapping it until we can get him out of country."

"Anyone else?" Stone glanced around at the other members of Hank's team.

"Nothing a little alcohol won't fix," Cole said.

"I swear I must have hit my head on my way up that hill," Stone said. "When everyone was bailing out of the cave, I counted one too many."

Hank looked around. "My six-man team is here."

"So's mine," Stone said.

Bubba raised a hand. "You counted right," he said and leaned back and shoved forward the lean figure dressed in black who'd been tucked between him and the far door of the aircraft. "Stone, we ran into this one rolling out of the back of an early morning delivery truck full of produce near the village east of our cave."

He pulled a ball cap off the man's head and a curtain of dark hair fell down around his shoulders.

When he looked up in the limited starlight shining in through the open door of the Black Hawk, it became obvious...

He wasn't a he at all. *He* was a *she*.

"Who the hell are you?" Stone demanded.

The woman lifted her chin. "Kyla Russell. I'm an American journalist."

# CHAPTER 3

K<small>YLA GAVE</small> the snarling man a big smile. "Thank you for getting me out of there."

The man's frown deepened, and he turned it on Bubba. "Explain."

"Like I said, she rolled off the back of a produce truck and would've been captured by Taliban soldiers had we not been there at that exact moment and hid her behind a pile of rocks."

"Why didn't you say anything when we were coordinating this effort?" Stone demanded.

"They found me early this morning," Kyla said.

Bubba nodded. "You were in the air. I couldn't tell you then."

"And you couldn't tell us as we landed and unloaded the Black Hawk?"

Kyla jumped in. "The Taliban arrived in the village shortly after Bubba and the gang found me. We spent the better part of the day making our way up to the cave without being seen."

"That's right. We didn't want the Taliban following us," Carter said.

Dax snorted. "Fat lot of good that did us. Someone had to have told them which direction we went."

Moe, his lips forming a thin line, nodded. "They probably tortured a few of the locals to get that information."

"Anyway," Hunter said. "We're stuck with her. She's an American. We have to take her, or she won't survive here."

Kyla gave Hunter a grateful grimace. "I'm sorry to be a bother, but I didn't think the Taliban would turn on all journalists so quickly."

"It's not just that you're a journalist," Hank said. "You're a female. I'm sure the Taliban doesn't want journalists reporting on how things are going for the women of Afghanistan, now that the Taliban is in charge again. They'd made a public statement that nothing would change."

"But it has." Kyla's jaw tightened. "I've seen what's happening. The schools for girls haven't reopened. They're having to teach underground, and the women who speak out are punished." She hoped her story rang true for these men. Her real mission for being in Afghanistan had nothing to do with journalism or reporting the current affairs in the lives of the Afghan people. They might not have been so generous including her in their escape from the country if they'd known what she really did for a living. Past tense. Now that she'd blown her last assignment, she doubted she could go back to her old job. And from the attacks in Kandahar, it would be a death sentence.

The helicopter slowed then hovered and slowly sank to the ground.

"I have more questions," Stone said.

"They'll have to wait." Hank nodded toward the C-17 airplane. "We have to stow the Hawk inside that bird and bug out, pronto."

Kyla was glad for the reprieve. Her escape from Kandahar had been a challenge.

As she and Bubba's men had climbed up to the cave, she'd looked back to see a Taliban truck full of rifle-toting gunmen enter the village. If they'd caught up with the truck, they would've seen her. They could've been after her, or the men who'd hidden her behind a rock pile. Or they were on a regular patrol, looking for infidels to exterminate.

The Taliban were the least of her worries. Two or three assassins, as well-trained in the art of killing as she was, were more lethal than a dozen Taliban fighters. She'd reneged on a job, and other assassins had been sent to do the job and tie up loose ends...namely her.

Not only had she refused to complete her assignment, she'd helped her target escape. Apparently, her handler had been serious about eliminating Ahmadi and hadn't trusted just one assassin to complete the task. Thus, her hurried departure from Kandahar. She hoped they were still looking for her there and hadn't expanded their search into the outlying countryside.

She could not have landed in the dirt at a more opportune set of boots. Bubba's guys had welcomed her and taken her under their wing.

Her gaze met Stone's.

Their boss...not so much. It didn't matter. She'd play the nice journalist as long as necessary to get a free ride back to the States. Then she'd have to figure out where she could hole up until she discovered the truth about the arms-dealing Abaddon and why they'd been tasked to kill Ahmadi, who might have been targeted for knowing too much and getting too close to a secret someone didn't want revealed. Someone in the government who'd sacrifice the lives of trained operatives to keep that secret hush-hush.

Once the helicopter landed, the men leaped out, and the crew went to work breaking it down and removing the rotors to fit the bird into the back of the C-17.

The man named Hank sent his able-bodied men out to assist with the perimeter guard. Stone put his men to work helping the Air Force C-17 and the Army Black Hawk crews load the chopper in the plane. The task was difficult. Kyla helped where she could, jumping in without being asked. The quicker the chopper was loaded, the sooner they could get in the air and out of range of the Taliban.

An agonizing hour later, the helicopter was in and secured, the men guarding the perimeter returned to the aircraft and the crew prepared the plane for take-off. As the ramp rose on the back of the plane, Kyla looked into the distance in the direction from which they'd come.

A plume of dust rose into the air, moving closer like a dirt devil, only this plume wasn't wind-induced. Instead, it was caused by what appeared to be a convoy of trucks, speeding toward them.

"We've got incoming." Stone claimed the jump seat next to Kyla's and secured his seatbelt.

Kyla counted the seconds as the ramp continued its slow progress until it closed.

The pilot had the engines running and ready. Once the ramp was secure. The plane lurched forward, gathering speed at what felt like a snail's pace.

With no windows to peer out, they had no idea if the plane was staying well enough ahead of the trucks racing toward them or if the men aboard those trucks had RPGs or other missile launchers capable of damaging the large aircraft.

As the plane left the ground, something rocked the fuselage. Kyla's pulse pounded through her veins. She reached out for something to hold onto and encountered Stone's hand.

His fingers curled around hers as the plane rose

into the air. As the aircraft leveled off, so too did Kyla's anxiety.

Flying was a necessary evil. She didn't like it, because she wasn't in control. It wasn't that she was particularly afraid, just unsettled because she could do nothing to influence the outcome of every takeoff and landing. She was at the mercy of others, a state in which she wasn't at all comfortable.

On her own feet, behind the wheel of a vehicle, even parachuting from the sky, she was pulling the strings, using her muscles and mind. She was in control.

"Are you okay?" Stone asked.

It wasn't until he spoke over the roar of the plane's engines that she realized she was still holding his warm, strong hand. Immediately, she released it, her cheeks heating as her fingers cooled. Strangely, she missed the feel of his bigger fingers wrapped around hers.

Kyla brushed the thought aside and pushed back her shoulders. "I'm good," she said and looked around. "I like it better when I can see out a window."

Stone nodded. "Same here. Especially when there's incoming enemy forces and we have no way of defending ourselves. I don't like it when I have no control over my destiny."

Kyla laughed. "Exactly." She smiled and held out her hand. "I haven't had a chance to thank you properly."

Once again, his hand closed around hers.

Without the pressing anxiety of the plane leaving the ground, Kyla felt an unexpected flash of electricity bolting up her arm. She blinked and met his gaze.

His brow dipped, and he stared at her hand. "Like I said, you don't have to thank me. You need to thank Hank. He's the one who pulled this mission together."

She nodded, her hand remaining in his. "From what Bubba said, you've been trying to get them out for weeks."

"I have. But it took Hank and his connections to pull off the extraction."

Kyla stared across the bay to where Hank sat on the other side with his team. The man leaned back in his seat with his arms crossed and his eyes closed, as if it was nothing for him to fly into enemy territory, rescue six people and fly back out, all under enemy fire.

Kyla shook her head. "Who is he that he can command that much sway with the military?"

Stone's lips quirked on both sides. "One of the best Navy SEALs to ever graduate BUD/S and go on to serve his country, doing what SEALs do."

"Risking their lives in some of the most dangerous missions." Kyla nodded. "I guess he made some friends along the way."

"He did. And he's only made more in his life as a civilian."

"He's not active duty?" She nodded toward Bubba. "I know your team isn't active, but I thought for sure

Hank's team was. How else did he get military backing to stage such a perilous mission?"

"His military service and his connections since," Stone said. "Now that our gig is up in Afghanistan, my security firm is out of business. We're hoping to go to work with Hank."

She cocked an eyebrow. "What's his business, besides rescuing people from untenable situations?"

Stone's lips twisted. "Just that. He's the owner, operator and brains behind Brotherhood Protectors, based in Montana. They provide security services to include bodyguard, protection, extraction and anything else most people don't have the skills to do. He hires only the best of the best of our former military—Navy SEALs, Army Rangers, Delta Force, Marine Force Reconnaissance and more."

"Wow," she said. "And the men on his team?"

"Are like him. Trained fighters who can do more than just fight. They can think on their feet, handle the stress of combat and danger and would do anything to protect those they're responsible for."

She chuckled. "You don't have to sell me on them. They sound like a dream team." Kyla met Stone's gaze. "Where do you fit in? Were you a Delta, Ranger, SEAL, etcetera?"

He raised a hand. "Navy SEAL. Hank and I fought together on a number of missions when we were on active duty. He got called home to Montana to help with the family ranch. When I separated from active duty, I chose to form my own security firm and hire out to the American companies helping rebuild infrastructure in Afghanistan." He tipped his head toward his team. "These are the last members of what was Stone Security. All my guys are prior-military, special operations fighting men like Hank and his group."

"You've been your own boss for a while." Kyla's brow furrowed. "How do you feel about going to work for someone else?"

"It's Hank." Stone gave her a quick smile. "He makes everyone feel like a part of the team, not like he's the boss and it's his way or the highway. He values his team's opinions and their ability to think on their feet and under stress."

She nodded. "Right. And he has connections."

"Not just that. He's a good person, who cares about people. He and his wife, Sadie McClain, fund the clients who can't pay for their services. If they need the Brotherhood, money isn't an issue."

Kyla stared across at the man called Hank Patterson. He was talking to one of his men. He laughed out loud and shook his head. He seemed like a genuinely nice man. "Sounds like he might be able to use you and your team."

"I hope so. They're good men. Civilian life is never an easy transition when you're trained to fight."

Kyla knew exactly what he meant. Too many people who'd seen high-intensity combat in the military couldn't make that transition. Too often they couldn't find a way to fit into their lives back home. Suicide became the only way out of their terrible frustration.

"I'm glad Hank's got work for our highly trained combatants." Kyla wondered if he hired females with similar skills.

No, she hadn't served in the military, but she had been in the CIA. Her special skills and training had landed her a position on the ultra-elite, secret organization designed to strategically target individuals at the crux of domestic and foreign problems resulting in the loss of innocent lives.

As good a guy as Hank was, he probably wouldn't want to touch an assassin.

But there might be room for a journalist with great communications skills. He didn't have to know the rest of her story. Not yet.

"He's based in Montana?"

Stone nodded. "Yes, ma'am. He has a satellite office in Colorado that's growing. And he has an agent in Hawaii. I'm hoping to convince him to open another satellite office on the border of Wyoming."

"Really?" She raised her eyebrows. "Near Cheyenne?"

He shook his head. "Yellowstone."

She smiled. "I admit I've never been there. I've always wanted to go to that part of the country. I've been to the west coast, but never Montana or Wyoming."

His lips pressed into a tight line. "Be careful what you wish for."

"Why do you say that?" Kyla asked.

"The original plan was to fly back to Germany where we picked up the Black Hawk and the C-17 for our mission. From there, Hank's chartered a plane to take us back to his place in Montana where my guys can decompress."

"From Germany to Montana?" Kyla shook her head.

"You might prefer to stay in Germany. Otherwise, you won't have another stop, except for fuel, until we get to Bozeman, Montana."

Kyla sat back in her jump seat, trying to hide how relieved that made her feel.

"Your news team might want you back sooner. I'm sure you can find a flight from Frankfurt to D.C., or wherever your company is based."

She shot him a weak smile. "Actually, I'm a free-lance journalist. My specialty had been Afghanistan." So, the journalist part of her story was a lie, but Afghanistan had been her area of expertise. She's been trained in the languages, customs, laws and political leaders of the government, and now, the Taliban. "Since Afghanistan is now under Taliban rule, I'm thinking I'm out of work."

"Where do you live when you're not on assignment?" Stone asked.

She snorted softly. "I gave up my apartment months ago. I was never there."

"What did you do with your things?"

Kyla held out her hands, palms up. "I travel light." She chuckled. "Well, not always this light. When I do rent an apartment, I get one fully furnished. That way I don't have to move furniture when I leave."

"I think we have a lot more in common than liking to be in control." He stared at the Black Hawk as if he was staring into the past. "I gave up my apartment a couple of years ago when I started my security service. I've been living out of hotels and vacation rentals ever since."

"I take it you're not married."

He shrugged. "What woman would put up with a man who's never home? I haven't been home in ten years."

"So, you do have a home?" she asked.

He nodded. "Well, my father has a place in the town where I grew up. For the past five years, he's been after me to come live with him."

"Is that town Yellowstone?" she asked.

He nodded. "West Yellowstone."

"Must have been a great place to spend your childhood."

Again, he nodded. "It was. I spent my summers riding horses, hiking, fishing and exploring the park and the surrounding mountains. My winters spent skiing, riding snowmobiles and playing in a winter wonderland." A soft smile formed on his lips, making the man's face soften from the hard angles and tight jaw of the man who'd been angry about her

41

addition to the rescue. Hell, that smile tugged at her heart, making her want to know this man even better.

"Sounds perfect," she said, and she didn't mean the town or the park. Her words reflected what she saw in the man. If she were in the market for a relationship... Yeah, she'd be tempted by this guy.

Stone had broad, muscular shoulders; he was strong, highly trained in combat skills and could probably hold his own in a fight with her, if any such event ever occurred.

A trill of excitement rippled through her at the thought. She'd never actually met a man who could hold his own physically with her. She swore she'd never consider falling for someone who wasn't her equal in many ways.

Deep down, she knew she'd formed that belief as a defense mechanism. Such a stance kept her from allowing herself to fall in love. When would she ever find a man equal in skills to her own? As an assassin, falling in love was out of the question. She had too many secrets, went on too many missions and never had time to give to someone else. And spending time with someone would only open her up to love and loss. Surely, no man would want to be with a woman who couldn't be with him so many days out of the year.

However, as of a day ago, when she'd helped a target escape termination, she was now unemployed and in need of a new career. Hadn't she already told herself...*no more killing*? She could start over. As long as her past remained in the past. In Montana or Wyoming, who could find her? Who would go to the effort?

With a new life, maybe she could finally let herself fall in love and find someone who could love her in return.

She glanced over at Stone. It was a stretch to think of this man as a potential candidate. They were strangers and barely knew each other.

Kyla leaned her head back and closed her eyes, a smile tugging at her lips.

If not Stone, then someone else. There had to be more men in Yellowstone.

But men she would consider an equal...?

Sure.

And pigs could fly. Still, a girl had to have dreams.

In the meantime, she had to find a job. And she would do the digging necessary to get the full story of why her organization had put a hit out on Ahmadi, and then tried to take her out as well.

Her chest tightened and, even though the air temperature was cool inside the plane, her palms began to sweat.

Too many variables were out of her control. She was in an airplane, sitting beside a cranky man who had an incredible smile and could be a candidate for the position of father of her baby.

Kyla's eyes popped open, and she sat up straight.

*Whoa, girl. Don't get ahead of yourself. You'll only set yourself up for failure.*

Her glance turned to the man beside her, and she sighed. "I could do worse," she murmured.

Stone frowned. "What did you say?"

"N-nothing," she stammered. "I'm going to rest my eyes. Wake me when we get close."

She had work to do before she entertained the idea of a real life. And what man...even one who had combat experience like Stone...would want to be with a female assassin? Some secrets would have to go with her to the grave.

And the grave was a distinct possibility if she didn't figure out what had gone so terribly wrong in Kandahar.

# CHAPTER 4

SLEEP WASN'T an option in a jump seat in the belly of a C-17. The noise was deafening, and there was no way to recline. Still, he'd managed to nod off several times. When his head lolled too far to the right the first time, he'd woken with a start to find Kyla's head resting against his shoulder, her silky black hair splayed over his body armor vest.

She smelled earthy, of dust and outdoors, a scent he found comforting and a little arousing. His thoughts went to standing in a shower with this woman, helping each other wash the dust of Afghanistan off their bodies.

Jesus! He'd been too long without a woman in his bed. His last girlfriend had been over three years ago, before he'd separated from the Navy. She'd lasted the month he'd been stateside between deployments. Once he'd left, she'd moved on to another man.

Stone's lip curled upward on one side. A gate guard at a retirement village.

The man didn't even have a weapon at his gate. Not that he needed one with the clientele who lived within the community. He'd probably shoot himself in the foot if he were given a loaded gun.

Not that Stone cared. He couldn't even remember the woman's name. In his work with the Navy SEALs, he'd come to expect the women in his life to be temporary distractions. Nothing more. He'd avoided long-term commitments like some of his buddies had attempted. Keyword: attempted. Too many of those had ended in divorce when they were gone more than they were home. Most relationships couldn't stand the test of time away.

Going from the Navy to owning his own security firm hadn't been anymore stable. He was still gone more than he was home and not to places he could take a girlfriend or spouse.

Now that he'd shut down his firm, he didn't have an excuse. But was he ready?

The woman beside him moved. Her head slid off his shoulder and down the front of his chest until she rested across his lap, her hair fanning out across his thighs.

Stone swallowed a groan. He really needed to get laid if having a dirty, dusty woman lying across his legs was a turn-on. It didn't help that her ear was aligned with his crotch, and his body's involuntary response was the hardening of his cock.

How could he move away from her without waking her? He glanced down at her face, the dark crescents of her eyelashes blending with the dark smudges beneath her eyes.

The journalist was not stunningly beautiful, but she wasn't a dog. Her jaw was a bit square, and she was a little taller than most of the women he usually dated. Her shoulder pressed against the side of his thigh was hard and muscular. He bet she'd give him a run for his money in an arm-wrestling contest.

Why was a journalist in such good shape? Working in a foreign country, when did she have time to hit the gym?

He wasn't sure, but her story that she was a journalist didn't seem to fit. Not that he'd dated a journalist or knew any personally. It was just a feeling. And if she wasn't a journalist, what had she been doing in Afghanistan? And why would she lie?

Unless she had something to hide.

Despite his growing shaft and discomfort, he didn't have the heart to move out from beneath her. She looked like she could use the sleep. And some food.

He took the opportunity to study her as she slept.

She had a couple of small fading scars. One on her forehead and another on her cheek, just below the corner of her eye.

Stone raised his hand, automatically reaching for the one on her cheek and wondering how she'd gotten it. Had she fallen on the playground as a kid?

Or had she been with a guy who'd liked to hit women?

His hand froze before he actually touched a finger to the scar. Instead, he brushed a strand of her hair back from her forehead and tucked it behind her ear.

The more he studied her, the more he realized his first observation had been incorrect. The woman was beautiful, in a strong striking way. To be a journalist willing to travel inside a country unfriendly with the ways of western women, she had to be strong and capable.

That she'd managed to stow away on the back of a produce truck showed some gumption. Her athletic ability had been obvious when she'd leaped over the edge of the cave entrance and controlled her slide down the slope to the bottom of the hill.

Stone hadn't done better. He was lucky he hadn't ended up with a broken neck.

He found himself wishing he could spend a little more time with this woman. She probably had some stories to tell with her time spent covering world events like the war in Afghanistan.

She had to be either brave or stupid to put herself in such risky situations, or a combination of both. Her brown-black eyes sparkled with intelligence as if she could read into a person's mind and extract all his deepest, darkest secrets.

Kyla hadn't said whether she'd leave them in Germany and make her way back to somewhere in the States other than Montana.

He found himself hoping she'd stay with them all the way to Hank's place. Given she didn't have a place of her own, it made sense. Unless she didn't have a place because she had a significant other who did. Unexpectedly, a stab of something like jealousy knifed him in the gut.

Why did he care? He didn't know her. Probably wouldn't see her ever again after she left them in Germany or Montana. Instead of getting hot over a woman, he should be thinking about the proposal he would make to Hank.

Where he went and what he did with his life hinged on Hank's answer. Not just Stone's future was at stake. With all his Afghan contracts canceled, he didn't have the funds to sustain his team. They didn't have work Stateside.

If Hank was as busy as he said he was, he could use additional staffing, and why not place it at another location like he had in Colorado?

Granted, Yellowstone wasn't that far from Eagle Rock, Montana, but it was far enough. And they could take on work in other areas besides Yellowstone and Wyoming. The only town close to Yellowstone National Park was West Yellowstone, Montana, located near the junction of Montana, Wyoming and Idaho.

His men were game and capable of traveling to their assignments. They just wanted jobs that paid a living wage. They didn't expect the inflated salaries they'd received in the war-torn country of

Afghanistan.

And he had the perfect location for a satellite office in Yellowstone. He just had to convince his father it was a good idea. It wasn't like his old man had guests year-round. They didn't keep horses anymore, and the old barn would work perfectly as an office once they remodeled the interior, stubbed in electricity, WIFI and a couple of living quarters with bathrooms. His guys could stay in the lodge until the barn renovations were complete.

He tore his gaze from the sleeping woman and met Hank's gaze across the bay.

Stone would be lying if he said he wouldn't mind working for someone else. But he hadn't lied about his opinion of Hank. Hank always brought out the best in the people around him. Even in leadership positions in the past, he'd taken suggestions from everyone to get things going. When tight on time, he wouldn't hesitate to bark out an order. He was decisive and fair.

Stone could work with or for Hank Patterson. He was a good man.

The corners of Hank's lips quirked.

The man had to know Stone was thinking about him. Hank was a fair guy. He'd hear him out, and then make a decision that would work for as many as possible without degrading the capabilities of their current staff.

A member of the Air Force crew walked down each side of the aircraft, softly notifying them that they'd be landing in ten minutes and to buckle their seatbelts if they weren't already fastened.

Stone shook Kyla's shoulder.

She popped upright, her head nearly connecting with Stone's jaw.

He jerked back in time to avoid a collision and chuckled. "Are you always this jumpy when you wake?"

Kyla blinked and stared around the bay as if refamiliarizing herself with her environment before she spoke.

Finally, she inhaled and released a long breath. "Yes. It's what keeps me alive."

Stone could definitely relate with the sentiment. "Well, I'm glad you got a little sleep."

Her eyes rounded, and she glanced down at his lap. "Was I...?"

"Asleep in my lap?" he grinned. "Yes."

She scrubbed her hands down her cheeks and back up to rub her eyes. "Did I snore or drool?"

"Not in the least."

"You should've woken me. I'm sure it couldn't have been comfortable to sit so long without moving."

"I'm not complaining." He tipped his head toward the back of his seat. "I never could sleep sitting up in one of these. Thankfully, the plane Hank chartered for us to fly back to the states is a lot more comfortable."

With her cheeks a soft shade of embarrassed pink, she grimaced. "I am sorry for inconveniencing you."

"Don't be. It can get cold in these planes at high altitudes. You kept me warm." He lifted his chin. "Now, check your belt and prepare for the landing."

Her body stiffened. "I'm such a wimp at flying. I actually like helicopters more because they can be left open. I can see outside."

"Have you flown in a helicopter many times covering stories?"

She hesitated for a moment before answering. "Yeah. A number of times."

The plane slowed. A couple of minutes later, the landing gear lowered and locked into place.

Stone reached across and claimed Kyla's hand.

He held it in his all the way to the ground and even as they taxied back to the terminal.

It wasn't until the C-17 came to a full stop, that he released his hold on her hand, and reluctantly at that. He found he liked holding her hand in his. She had a strong grip, yet her fingers were long and feminine.

Stone hoped Kyla and Hank could come to a satisfactory agreement as to where she would leave them.

Montana would be Stone's choice.

There was still so much he didn't know about this woman who had braved a hostile country to get a story. The long flight back wouldn't be enough time to dig deeper. He suspected there was a lot more to her than she displayed on the surface, and he wanted to know it all.

How had she managed to move around Afghanistan without wearing the required black abaya? And why was she dressed like a cat burglar, with her black shirt and pants? She was lucky his team had found her when they had. The Taliban wouldn't have been in the least sympathetic to her lack of respect for their laws.

Though she'd squeezed his hand during the takeoff and landing, she wasn't a weak woman. She'd worked alongside his team and the aircraft crews to prepare the chopper for transport. Some of the items she'd carried were heavy, yet she'd made it look easy.

Once the aircraft came to a stop, Stone unbuckled his seatbelt and stood, working the kinks out of muscles after being still for too long.

Kyla rose next to him and stretched her arms above her head. The movement pulled her shirt tight across her breasts. Though dressed in dark pants and a dark shirt, there was no denying she was a female, with subtle curves in all the right places. Her body was more athletic than curvaceous.

Once the aircraft engines shut down, Hank crossed the aircraft's floor to stand in front of Kyla and Stone.

"I'm taking Zach to the hospital at Landstuhl. He'll fly back on a commercial airline when he's recovered enough. While we're at Landstuhl, the rest of you will be transported to the general aviation airport where the charter jet is waiting to take us back to the states."

His gaze met Kyla's. "What are your plans, Ms. Russell? Are you leaving us here? If you stay with us, we're flying from here straight to Bozeman, Montana, with only a short fuel stop in Halifax, Nova Scotia. No one is getting off at that point. So, it's here or Bozeman."

She blew out a breath. "You didn't expect to transport an extra body on your mission. Are you sure you have the load capacity on the aircraft?"

Hank gave her a gentle smile. "Positive. It's not like you're carrying a ton of extra baggage like my wife, Sadie, would."

"That's true." Kyla grinned and lifted her palms. "What you see is what you get."

Stone liked when she smiled. Her expression was often too serious, with fine lines around her eyes and mouth that weren't from smiling. When she smiled, her dark eyes shone, making Stone's heartbeat stutter.

Her eyes narrowed. "Did I hear Stone correctly? Is your wife Sadie McClain the movie star?"

Hank nodded. "She is."

"Wow. She's amazing."

"Yes, she is," Hank said with a smile. "I don't know what she sees in me. I'm the luckiest man alive."

Stone felt a tug of envy at the love for his wife shining from Hank's eyes. He was almost a different man from the one who'd fought alongside him in

Iraq and Afghanistan years before. Stone was glad for his friend. He deserved happiness after all he'd given for his country.

Maybe someday, Stone would find that same happiness and peace Hank had found.

The ramp lowered at the back of the C-17, and headlights shone into the interior from three large black passenger vans pulled up behind the plane.

"So, what's it going to be?" Hank asked Kyla.

"If you're okay with me tagging along, I've never been to Montana. I've come this far with you and your team; I'd like to go the rest of the way with you."

He gave her a nod. "Good. Then I'll see you at the charter plane as soon as I get Zach settled."

Bubba stepped up beside Kyla. "Glad you're coming with us. We kind of feel responsible for you since we found you in the village."

Kyla smiled. "Thanks, Bubba. I'm glad I bumped into you. It would've taken me a lot longer to get out of the country if it weren't for all of you."

Stone couldn't imagine what other challenges she might have faced maneuvering through Afghanistan as an unaccompanied female. That she'd made it as far as she had was a testament to her bravery and resilience.

"I've arranged for you all to use the facilities at the terminal," Hank said. "I also ordered food to be delivered. Save me some. I'll be there as soon as I can."

"Does the crew need us to help unload the Black Hawk?" Kyla asked.

Hank shook his head. "They want to wait until daylight and for the maintenance crew to handle it. We're cleared to go."

The men filed out of the plane and climbed into the vans.

Stone and Kyla followed members of Stone's team to the last van. Bubba claimed the front passenger seat. Carter and Dax climbed into the seat at the very back. Hunter and Moe took the seat in front of them. Kyla slid onto the middle bench and scooted over. Stone settled on the seat beside her. Like Bubba, he felt responsible for the woman and wanted to be sure she arrived safely back in the States.

Two of the vans left the base headed for the airfield where the chartered jet waited. Hank's van with the injured man turned toward the hospital at Landstuhl.

"I hope he's going to be all right," Kyla said.

"They have excellent doctors at Landstuhl," Stone said. "He'll be back in the States in no time."

"Especially if Hank has anything to say about it," Bubba said over his shoulder.

"That's right. The man can move mountains," Stone said. "I should've contacted him sooner."

Moe reached over the back of Stone's seat and clamped a hand on his shoulder. "We made it out. That's all that counts."

"Yeah. And I can't wait to get my lips around a big juicy hamburger," Dax said.

Hunter groaned. "Drooling here. Could you save

voicing your dream food until we get close enough to satisfy your craving?"

"How long has it been since you've had a decent meal?" Kyla asked.

"Since we arrived in Afghanistan," Dax said. "MREs don't count."

"At least we had some to get us by," Bubba reminded them.

"I'm not complaining," Dax said. "Not much, anyway. We're on our way home."

"Home…" Carter sighed. "What's that? You realize we're jobless, homeless and have to start over?"

"I look at it as an opportunity to reinvent ourselves," Bubba said.

"Bubba," Dax snorted, "ever the optimist."

"Hey, I know you're probably feeling a bit adrift," Stone said. "I'm in the same boat. Our work was in Afghanistan."

"Now, it's not," Carter said.

"Right," Stone said. "But I'm working on it."

"What can we do stateside? Form our own construction company?" Dax asked. "I'm dead-on with an M4A1 rifle. I suck with a nail gun."

"We're heading for Hank's ranch in Montana," Stone continued. "I've got ideas I want to explore."

"How long will we be there?" Bubba asked.

"I hope only a couple of days, tops," Stone said. He was ready to move on to Yellowstone. Having been gone a decade, he was finally ready to go home. His father had been out to see him a couple of times when he'd still been in the service. Both times in San Diego where he'd been stationed. That had been nearly five years ago.

The old man wasn't getting any younger. Stone wanted time with his father. He wouldn't be around forever. Pulling out of Afghanistan was the catalyst that had forced him to rethink his life's trajectory. He also felt obligated out of loyalty and respect to help the men who'd believed in him find rewarding and satisfying work. If not with him, then with someone who would value their skills. Someone like Hank Patterson.

"Will a couple of days at Hank's ranch give us enough time to explore your ideas?" Bubba asked. "Should we be hitting the help-wanted ads in the meantime?"

"No," Stone said. "I've got money set aside in my business account. I can pay you guys for a couple of months until we get something started or until we all find another opportunity."

Bubba glanced over his shoulder at Stone, his eyes narrowed. "If I'm not working, I'm not drawing a paycheck from Stone Securities. I have money of my own. I can go for a couple of months until I find a job."

"I think it's the same for all of us," Hunter said. "We didn't have anywhere to spend our paychecks in Afghanistan. It's been piling up in the bank. We don't need you to float us while we're figuring things out."

Stone's heart swelled. "Hopefully, we'll be working within the next couple of weeks."

"You gonna let us in on what you have in mind?" Dax asked from the back of the van.

"I don't want to say anything yet. I don't know if my idea will float. Give me a couple of days."

His team made him proud. They were the brothers he'd never had growing up. Stone wanted to keep them together, if at all possible.

The vans pulled into a small airport and stopped in front of the door. Stone recognized it as the terminal where they'd landed two days before they'd launched their extraction mission.

"This is our stop," he said and slid the side door open. He got out and held out his hand for Kyla.

She glanced at his hand with a wrinkled brow and then placed hers in his. "I'm capable of getting out of a vehicle on my own."

Bubba chuckled. "We witnessed her abilities. You'll want to help her down."

The other men added to Bubba's laughter.

Kyla gave a crooked grin. "You try launching yourself off a stack of oranges."

Bubba held up his hands. "No thanks. We'll leave that to the expert."

"At least I didn't break anything," she said. "That should count for something."

"It does," Carter said. "Hey, Stone, when you come up with our next venture, you should find a place for our mascot."

"Mascot?" Stone asked.

Carter waved a hand toward Kyla. "Ms. Russell. We can't leave our mascot out of the fun."

Stone wouldn't admit he'd been racking his brain for something Kyla could do. How could she fit into the Brotherhood Protectors if he managed to convince Hank to set up another office in Yellowstone?

"She's a journalist," Stone said. "I'm sure she has better things to do with that training than hang out with a bunch of meat grinders like us."

"I'm here, you know," she murmured. "It's not like I'm in a different room."

"Yeah, Stone. Let her speak for herself," Carter said.

Stone turned to Kyla. "We're more or less mercenaries who provide security for people and businesses. How would a journalist fit into that picture? I wish you'd tell me because I haven't been able to come up with a thing."

She smiled and patted his cheek. "You'd be surprised." Then she looked past him to the terminal. "Right now, though, I'd love a shower and food."

"Same here," Bubba said. "How about a little more action and lot less talk?" he held out his arm toward Kyla.

She hooked her hand through the crook of his elbow and marched into the terminal with the big guy.

Stone frowned, that surge of heat and anger

pushing through his veins surprising him more than he cared to acknowledge.

Kyla had spent the past few hours sitting beside him on the plane, holding his hand when she was nervous and talking to him. Why the hell was she walking away with Bubba instead of him?

Moe leaned close to Stone and chuckled. "I think you pissed her off."

Stone's frown deepened. "How?"

"By talking as if she weren't right in front of you." Moe grinned. "That girl has spunk. Think she'd go out with a guy like me?"

Dax punched Moe in the arm. "Dream on, dude. A woman like that likes a man she can look up to."

Moe glared up at Dax who stood three inches taller. "Fuck you. Just because you're taller doesn't mean you're better. I have skills the ladies love." He lifted his chin, pushed past Dax and entered the terminal.

Stone shook his head. These men had been in a country where the women were off-limits. They needed time to blow off a little steam and decompress. Back in the States, they'd have the opportunity to meet women, date and, maybe, fall in love.

Just not with Kyla.

Stone clenched his fists and marched toward the entrance to the terminal, determined to...what?

Fight Bubba for Kyla's attention?

Man, he needed to get some sleep. He was delirious thinking about this woman he barely knew.

Like the rest of his team, he needed to decompress and start working on a plan for his life before he fell for the first woman he'd spent more than an hour with in the past year or so.

*Damn.*

How long had it been since he'd gone on an honest-to-goodness date? He shook his head as he pushed through the door.

*Obviously, too long.*

A woman stood just inside the door and directed him toward the crew quarters where he could shower. Once they were ready, food would be served in the crew conference room.

Kyla and Bubba were nowhere to be seen, probably already in a shower. Hopefully, separate showers.

They had a long flight ahead of them to get to Bozeman, Montana. Stone would start with a cold shower to tamp down his libido and get his head on straight.

# CHAPTER 5

KYLA WAS SO happy to get into the shower, she'd stripped and ducked in even before the water warmed. The cool spray hit her skin, shocking her back into her senses.

The time she'd spent on the plane beside Stone had been weird. She'd never relaxed so much in a man's company, yet at the same time felt a tension that made her hyper-aware of his every move.

She'd marched off with Bubba to get away from Stone and the sensations his presence inspired inside her.

What was wrong with her?

Kyla turned her face into the spray, her body shivering until the water warmed. She turned, squirted shampoo into her hands and scrubbed her hair as if she could wash the feelings away. At first, it worked. But when she tipped her head back and rinsed out the suds, the warm water sluiced over her body and across her breasts, reminding her that she hadn't been touched there by a man in a very long time.

She raised her hands to tweak the tips of her nipples, making them form tight little beads. What would it be like to have Stone's bigger, callused hands brushing across her breasts?

A moan rose up in her throat and escaped before she could stop it.

"You all right in there?" that deep, familiar voice called out.

"I'm fine." Kyla squeaked, her body responding to Stone's tone. She straightened, her gaze going to the lock on the door. Had she engaged the mechanism? It appeared to be in the locked position. The problem was that she couldn't decide if she was relieved or disappointed. Had she left the door unlocked, she could have invited Stone to join her and pick up where she'd left off.

"Hank had clean clothes delivered," he said, his voice muffled. "I'm setting them down on the floor outside our door."

"Thank you," she said.

"Thank Hank," he shot back.

Hank had thought of everything. Kyla hadn't. So relieved to wash the dirt out of her hair and off her skin, she'd forgotten that she'd come with only the clothes on her back.

Knowing there was a limited number of showers for Stone and Hank's teams, she quickly washed her body, rinsed and stepped out of the shower. After running a towel over her body, she wrapped it around her, covering all the important parts. Easing open the door, she reached out, gathered what Stone had left and ducked back into the bathroom. She shook out a green flight suit like those that had been worn by the helicopter crew.

She smiled, slipped her legs in, pulled the suit up over her body and zipped it up the front. At five feet seven inches, she wasn't a small woman. But the suit hung on her, a couple sizes too big. Kyla didn't care. It was clean and dry. What more could she ask for? Hank had also provided clean socks. Again…too big, but warm and dry. She slipped into them and pulled on her boots.

After gathering her dirty clothes, she emptied the pockets, found a clean plastic bag and stuffed them inside. She would need them eventually, uncertain when she'd have time to shop for new clothes. Hopefully, she could get a few things in Bozeman.

The bathroom had drawers full of essential toiletries. Kyla found a brush, toothbrush and a travel-sized tube of toothpaste still in their initial packaging. She quickly brushed the tangles from her damp hair and slicked it straight back from her forehead. After she'd brushed her teeth, she slipped the items into her pockets, along with her passport. Then she grabbed her bag and left the bathroom as neat as when she'd entered it.

One of Hank's team, a man with black hair and blue eyes waited outside the door. Kyla remembered

Hank introducing him as Kujo. She smiled. "It's all yours."

"Thanks." He stepped to the side, allowing her to pass, then entered the bathroom and closed the door behind him. A man of few words.

Kyla was okay with that. The less she said, the less likely she'd slip up and reveal too much about herself. Thankfully, the number of people she'd killed should never come up in casual conversation. Her time in the CIA and with her current organization had taught her to keep secrets. Her life depended on it.

The special team of assassins she'd been recruited for was so secretive she didn't know any of the other members. And that was on purpose. That way, if she were captured and tortured, she couldn't reveal the names or descriptions of the other members. She'd never met her handler face to face. Her assignments had come to her over her phone or via specially delivered packages.

Up until her last assignment, she'd been all right with the setup. But once she'd become the target, she wasn't okay with not knowing who she could trust.

With Stone and Hank's teams, she felt she could trust them. They hadn't tried to kill her. They'd had their own issues to deal with, getting out of Afghanistan before the Taliban caught up with them.

She was glad she'd be traveling to Montana with them. Hopefully, she could continue on to Hank's ranch, if she could convince them she was of some value to Hank's or Stone's teams. A ranch out in the wilds of Montana would isolate her enough that she wouldn't have to look over her shoulder every time she left the house.

She needed time with a computer on the internet to do the digging necessary to find out who had given the order to kill Ahmadi and why. And who was this guy Abaddon? If she could nail that information, she might determine who was after her as well. The more she thought about it, the more she suspected that while she'd been sent to kill Ahmadi, the other assassins had been sent to kill her to tie up loose ends.

She needed to stay hidden in the boondocks with access to the internet long enough to get answers. The assassins who'd been after her couldn't know she'd hitched a ride in the back of a produce truck, much less that she'd fallen in with a daring extraction team. That should buy her some time. Hopefully enough.

And if she got to spend some time with Stone... bonus. She might actually get to scratch that itch and get it out of her system.

It wasn't like she was a regular person who could have a real life, settle down with a nice man and raise a family. When she'd chosen the career path of an assassin, she'd chosen to be alone for the rest of her life. The kinds of secrets she had stored in her memories weren't the kind that made for a stable relationship. She never knew if any of her assignments would come back to haunt her.

What if a relative of one of her hits decided to track down the sniper who'd picked off his brother, cousin or lover? She'd been careful with each tasking to make it clean. No witnesses. But after Kandahar, she didn't trust the very organization she'd worked for. She might not know them, but they knew her.

When she'd introduced herself to Bubba and the rest of Stone's team, she'd used the name on her fake passport, the one she'd had made on her own. Her handler had provided several passports for her use to get in and out of different countries. And she had used them. Thankfully, she'd had the foresight to acquire another passport only she knew about, with a name her organization wouldn't recognize. They wouldn't be able to trace it or her by the name Kyla Russell.

Now, facial recognition software was another matter entirely. With so many cameras positioned in public places, she could be spotted. She'd have to be careful. She'd pick up a hat somewhere, and when she had a chance, get some modeling wax if she needed to temporarily change the shape of her face.

She found Stone, Carter and Bubba in a large conference room, wearing similar attire to hers. The table held trays of food that had been laid out in the center. The food was typical German fare, including wiener schnitzel, goulash, bratwurst and other items Kyla couldn't identify. She didn't care. It smelled good, and she was hungry.

Stone passed her a paper plate.

Kyla helped herself to a little bit of everything, adding an extra spoonful of her favorite...goulash.

Stone chuckled. "Don't miss the strudel." He shoved a pan of apple strudel toward her.

"Thanks." She helped herself to a spoonful of the dessert, and then settled back to eat.

As the others finished their showers, they gathered around the table in their flight suits talking and laughing, going over the extraction and what they would have done differently.

Kujo shook his head. "Never thought I'd return to Afghanistan after I left the Army."

Bubba laughed. "We never thought we'd get out." His smile faded. "Thanks again. You all didn't have to. But you did."

"Couldn't leave some of our own there," Boomer added between bites of schnitzel.

By the time most of them had finished eating, Hank appeared, wearing a clean flight suit, his hair damp from a shower. "Did you save me any?" He grabbed a plate and helped himself to everything, adding a huge helping of the apple strudel. "I don't get to eat like this often. Sadie's trying to get me to eat healthy." He shuddered. "I can only take so much before I have to go out for a hamburger and fries."

Stone's team laughed.

Hank looked up, his brow wrinkling. "What?"

Dax shook his head. "As we were driving over from the base, I was telling the guys what I wanted first when I got back to the States." He grinned. "A big, juicy hamburger."

Hank nodded. "Since you're coming to the ranch, I know just the place. I'm pretty good at the grill, but steaks are my specialty. The Blue Moose Tavern in Eagle Rock makes a killer burger with anything you want on it. I like all the usual, along with a healthy portion of crispy bacon."

Dax groaned, leaning back in his chair with his hand on his flat belly. "You're killing me."

"Let's get there, and it'll be my treat."

Dax held up his hand. "I'm in."

The rest of Stone's team spoke as one, "Me, too."

Kyla smiled. She understood the simple pleasures. For Dax, it was a hamburger. For her, it was a hot fudge sundae. She turned to Hank.

"You don't have to wait on me," Hank said. "You can go on out to the plane and settle in, if you like."

Stone shook his head. "We'll be on that plane for eleven to twelve hours or more. I'd rather keep my feet on the ground as long as possible."

"After being holed up in a cave for days, I can wait to get into the confines of a plane," Bubba said.

"How's Zach?" Stone asked.

Hank chewed and swallowed before he answered. "Getting great care from the team of doctors and nurses at Landstuhl. The doctor said if he doesn't show any signs of infection, he'll be able to fly back the day after tomorrow. I have my computer guy, Swede, arranging his flight. He wanted to come with us, but I'd rather err on the safe side."

"I'm glad he'll be okay," Stone said.

Hank finished the last bite of strudel and pushed back from the table. "If you're ready, we can get this party started."

"I'm ready," Stone said. "Let's go home."

"Yeah," Moe agreed. "Let's go home."

"To home," Hunter called out.

Both teams shouted, "To home."

Moe clapped a hand on Stone's back and added, "Wherever that might be."

Kyla's thoughts echoed Moe's words. She hadn't known a true home since her parents had died and she'd been handed over to the state when she was ten years old. She'd been moved around from one foster family to another. That was where she'd learned not to get attached to things. It was easier to move if she didn't have to pack.

Anytime she'd moved, she'd been given a plastic trash bag in which to carry all of her belongings. She'd always felt she was being put out with the trash.

Thankfully, at fourteen, she'd made her last move in the foster care system, landing with a kind older couple, Jim and Carol, who'd given her the love and attention she'd always craved. They'd helped her to realize she could do anything she set her mind to. When she'd told them that one day she wanted to work for the CIA, they'd helped her research the requirements and had made certain she'd had the grades in school to get into the college of her choice. Because of them, she'd worked hard and realized her dream.

They'd been so proud of her.

And then a drunk driver had rear-ended them on the highway. Their car spun into oncoming traffic. They'd been hit head-on by an eighteen-wheeler.

Kyla had been so focused on making her mark in the CIA, she hadn't dated or made many friends, other than the few within the agency who could help her. Jim and Carol were all the family she'd had. And like her birth parents, they were gone, leaving her alone in the world.

Not long after that, she'd been recruited for her "special" assignment to the secret group of assassins. With no one to hold her back, no family who cared about her, or whom she cared about, she'd had nothing to lose.

Following Stone out onto the tarmac, Kyla almost stopped and turned around. These men were friends, had served together and had become family to each other.

Kyla hadn't realized just how much she missed having a family until she'd seen how these men interacted. They picked at each other, laughed and joked, but when the going got tough, they pooled their strength and helped their brothers through it.

Hell, Stone and Hank's team had flown halfway around the world, jumped through some significant hoops and risked being killed to rescue five of their men. They cared like family.

She didn't belong with them. Hadn't she learned by now that, for her, family didn't last? Travel light and don't get attached. That way you don't get hurt.

Watching Stone laughing and smiling scared Kyla. Anything she might discover with Stone had hurt written all over it. He was the kind of man who would eventually settle down, find a nice woman and have half a dozen children.

She couldn't begrudge him that life. And she sure as hell couldn't give it to him. Nice wasn't her. Assassins weren't nice. They were killers. She was a killer.

Her footsteps faltered, and she hung back. She was insane to think she could tag along with this happy group of men. She was the outsider. The one who didn't belong. The sooner she cut ties, the better off she'd be. The better off they'd be as well. Why complicate her life any more than it was?

Travel light, physically as well as emotionally.

She was just about to turn around when Stone reached the bottom of the stairs leading up into the jet. He turned, his gaze met hers and he held out his hand.

*Walk away, girl.*

"Hey." Stone smiled. "It's okay. I've got you."

Kyla's feet carried her toward him as if they had a mind of their own. Her hand reached for his.

With her head telling her it was a mistake, her heart overruled and sent her up the stairs and into the scariest place she'd ever been. A place filled with the potential of loss.

*There is always loss.*

And danger.

*Danger of caring too much.*

And risk.

*Of losing my heart.*

# CHAPTER 6

STONE HELD Kyla's hand through the take-off and well after the plane leveled off. As the seats had filled near the front of the plane, he and Kyla had settled near the rear.

When they'd been about to board, he'd looked back to see Kyla hesitate. At the time, he'd suspected she wasn't keen on flying again so soon after their last flight.

Once on board, her silence seemed to be more than her anxiety over flying. Her brow had a slight pucker, and her gaze didn't meet his for long before she looked away.

What had changed from the time she'd scarfed down apple strudel to the time she'd walked out onto the tarmac?

Was she second-guessing her decision to fly all the way to Montana with them?

Then again, she could be tired. They all were after the stress of escaping the Taliban.

Once the plane was in the air, the flight attendant offered the passengers blankets and pillows and then dimmed the interior lights.

Each of the seats on the chartered plane reclined fully with raised footrests.

Kyla extended her seat, tucked a pillow beneath her head, wrapped a blanket around herself and closed her eyes.

Stone had selfishly hoped they could talk for a few minutes before sleeping. He had so many questions for the journalist about her life, her work...everything.

Instead, he reclined his seat and crossed his arms over his chest, settling in for the long flight across the Atlantic.

When they got to Hank and Sadie's ranch, he had to present his idea to Hank and pray his friend was as excited about the collaboration as he was. His men needed the work, and Stone needed Hank and his connections Stateside.

Once he had a decision, he would figure out what was next for him and Kyla. Assuming she was coming with them to the ranch.

He hadn't considered she might be leaving them once they touched down in Bozeman. Hank hadn't actually invited her to stay at the ranch as he had Stone and his team.

He turned toward Kyla, wondering why he was so

drawn to the woman. Her dark hair had started to dry, and a strand had slipped forward, curling softly around her face, making her appear even more feminine and a little vulnerable.

Stone wanted to reach out and touch that silken strand and determine if it was as silky soft as it appeared.

Kyla's eyes fluttered open, her gaze connecting with his. A flush of pink filled her cheeks. "Why are you staring at me? Do I have goulash on my face?"

He smiled. "No. Sorry. I was just wondering what …" he struggled for a thought other than the texture of her hair, "is next for you, now that you're not covering Afghanistan."

She sighed. "If I only knew."

"Have you thought about pursuing another career?"

"Definitely," she answered. "Many times over the past few years."

He shook his head, smiling gently. So tempted to reach for that strand of hair. "Don't you like what you do?"

"Not really."

"I thought being a journalist was a calling. That telling a story was what you lived for."

"I thought it would be more…black and white."

Stone frowned. "What do you mean?"

"That in each assignment…story…you could identify an obvious right and wrong. The more…

assignments I covered...the more blurred the lines became, the more the black and white turned gray."

"I guess there are always two sides to every story."

She stared up at the ceiling, her eyes narrowing. "You just have to be careful to get all the information from both sides so you don't act on misleading information. And you can't always trust your sources."

"Sounds like you might have been burned before."

She nodded and turned to face him. "I have."

"So, why don't you do something different?"

"I'm going to," she said. "I just don't know what that something is."

"Is there anything else you've dreamed of doing besides being a journalist?" he asked.

"Not really."

"What are you good at? What skills can you draw on?"

She continued to stare up at the ceiling, a wry smile tipping the corners of her lips. "None that I care to use. I'm tired of k-what I do. I'm ready for a change. It's just hard when you're trained to do one thing to reimagine yourself."

Stone couldn't agree with her more. "I know exactly what you mean. When I left the Navy, I only knew one thing. How to fight and kill."

"It's amazing what we have in common," she murmured and followed quickly with, "the knowing one thing part."

Stone nodded. "I wasn't sure how I could transfer my combat training into a civilian job. The security business I set up was more or less an extension of what I'd done on active duty with a little less emphasis on killing and more on protecting. But it was still in a war-torn country, not one at peace like the US. I'm hoping we can make a smooth transition back home."

"You and me both." She sighed. "I just don't see how that can be possible," she whispered so softly, Stone barely caught her words.

"Have you been covering foreign stories for long?"

"Long enough."

"How long has it been since you've been home?"

She closed her eyes. "Forever."

The way Kyla said the one word made Stone's chest tighten.

"Where is home?" he asked quietly.

She shrugged. "I don't have one." She turned on her side, away from him. "Wake me when we're about to land to refuel...?"

"Sure." Stone studied her back as she lay beside him.

Her body was stiff, not relaxed like someone going to sleep.

He'd struck a sore spot when he'd asked her where home was. As long as it had been since he'd been to his own home, he'd always known it was there, and that his father was waiting for him to return.

His heart squeezed hard in his chest. What did it

feel like to have no home? No place to go to? No roots to ground you?

He didn't know, nor did he want to find out. His idea was to make his home the base of his operations. Stone had been away long enough.

Having a home to go to made him sad for Kyla, who had none, and made him want even more for her to come with him. She could start her new career in Yellowstone. Surely, she had a skill she could use to start her new career.

Stone lay for a long time, staring up at the ceiling of the aircraft.

Other than the sound of the plane's engines and one of the guys snoring softly, the interior of the plane was silent, allowing him to think.

After a while, he tried to clear his mind of the task ahead and his meeting with Hank. He succeeded only in falling into thoughts of Kyla and her homelessness.

Hell, at the very least, he could offer her a place to stay at his father's lodge until she figured out what she wanted to do next in her life. At least, that would give him an excuse to take her out to Hank's ranch until he headed southwest toward Wyoming.

Stone wasn't sure why he was hanging onto this woman, but something about her struck a chord with him. She'd seemed so strong and brave when he'd first met her. But under that brave exterior was a sadness and vulnerability he bet she'd deny if anyone pointed it out.

She made him want to protect her and to learn all

there was to know about her. He hoped she'd give him the chance to do just that.

It might not lead to anything, but his curiosity would be appeased, and she might have time to decide what career to pursue next. And what better, more beautiful and peaceful place than Yellowstone?

He fell asleep with a smile on his face in anticipation of going home and showing Kyla around the town that had made him who he was.

STONE WOKE Kyla when they landed briefly in Halifax, Nova Scotia, to refuel. They were only on the ground long enough to fill up on aviation fuel. The flight attendant offered snacks and drinks while they waited. Some of the men remained asleep throughout the layover.

Kyla didn't understand that at all. How could they be so relaxed when the big bus of an airplane was hurtling toward the ground and back into the air?

She knew it was just her phobia, but it didn't make it any less disturbing. Once they landed in Bozeman, she'd be back on the ground and in control of her destiny.

After the fuel truck left, the pilot taxied out onto the runway, and they were back in the air on the last leg of their flight to Montana.

Stone held her hand on the landing and take-off in Halifax, easing her anxiety and making her feel safe.

She drifted to sleep, facing Stone and still holding his hand, and she didn't wake until the cabin lights came on and the pilot announced they would be landing soon in Bozeman.

Kyla sat up straight and lifted the shade on the window. Outside, the sun was rising on a brand-new day. She stood and made her way to the lavatory to empty her bladder and brush her teeth. One glance in the mirror made her gasp and reach for her brush. When she emerged, she felt a little better. She wouldn't feel one hundred percent until her feet were firmly on the ground.

Stone and Hank were standing in the aisle talking when she returned to her seat.

Stone dropped into his chair and buckled his belt across his lap. Then he reached for her hand and glanced across at her. "All right?"

She nodded, her grip tightening around his fingers as the landing gear locked in place beneath the plane.

"I spoke with Hank," Stone said. "He'd like for you to stay at the ranch with us while we're there."

Kyla met Stone's gaze. "He does?"

Stone nodded. "I figure it'll give you some time to regroup."

She nodded. "That's nice of him to welcome a stranger into his home. Will his wife mind?"

Stone chuckled. "He said she would be excited to have female company."

Once again, Kyla fought an internal war between

her heart and head. Again, her heart won over her head. "I'd like that. It would give me a day or two to find a more permanent place to land."

"Right," Stone said. "Same for me."

"I thought you were headed for Yellowstone and home?" she said.

"I am, but I'm not sure yet if I'll be staying or just visiting. It all depends on some decisions that need to be made."

"I hope, for your sake, you get to make it permanent." She gave him a soft smile. "That seems to be where your heart is." Her chest hurt with the thought of Stone heading south and herself moving on to wherever she could find work.

*Doing what?*

The hell if she knew. What did a former assassin do after ending a killer career?

Fortunately, she'd been smart enough to bank her pay and invest in the stock market. Getting to it, might be a challenge. What she needed was to disappear, fade into the background, or the backwoods, and find something useful to do that would help people instead of hurting them. She was done with playing the role of executioner.

Not one to sit around and do nothing, she'd have to find gainful employment to keep her busy. Bozeman was a decent-sized town. She could apply for work there.

Or she could look for work in Yellowstone.

How would Stone feel if she followed him? Would

he think it creepy? At that moment, he was the closest thing to a friend she'd ever had. In her line of work, making friends wasn't advised. Contacts...yes. Friends...no. Friends and loved ones left you vulnerable. Someone could use them to get to her.

She didn't begin to believe she could just walk away from her job as an assassin employed by her federal government. They probably had some protocol for leaving the fold. After what had happened in Afghanistan, she was beginning to think that protocol was to kill the assassin so she couldn't talk about her work or targets to anyone else.

Unless someone in the organization had gone rogue and didn't want her to talk about the hit on Ahmadi. None of her other jobs had ended the way Kandahar had. She'd walked away on them. No one had tried to stop her or permanently silence her.

Could someone have gone bad in the secret organization? Was it her handler? Or was it the big boss who determined which assassin received certain assignments?

For the years she'd been working in the secret organization, she'd been careful not to dig deeper. She'd been given strict guidelines about contacting other members of the group. Contact between them was strictly forbidden, under the penalty of death.

Considering the nature of their work, it had seemed the right thing to do, and she'd stuck to her commitment to follow the rules.

Once she'd become the target, all bets were off.

All promises broken. If she wanted to survive, she had to find out who had put the hit out on her. And to do that, she had to find out why and who had decided Ahmadi was a threat.

She itched to find a computer and start her online search for answers. Until they landed in Montana, she could do nothing. Once there, a computer would be at the top of her list of needs.

Second would be clothes that fit better and didn't make her stand out like a kid playing dress-up in her dad's clothes.

While Stone dozed in the seat beside her, Kyla thumbed through magazines and newspapers the flight attendant had provided. When nothing caught her attention, she left her seat and stretched her legs, walking up and down the middle aisle of the plane.

On her second pass, Hank lifted a hand and motioned toward the empty seat beside him.

The pilot announced, "Please take your seats and fasten your seatbelts for the landing."

Kyla eased into the seat and buckled her seatbelt. "Thank you for offering to let me stay at your ranch while Stone's team is there."

Hank nodded. "Sadie will be excited to have another woman in the house. Though she loves to escape to the ranch, it can be lonely at times. Not that she's not completely busy taking care of our kids."

"I hope she won't be too disappointed. I won't have anything to contribute to a conversation about children and child-raising." She grinned. "Or making movies. I am interested in hearing about each, though." She'd never pictured herself having children.

"Most people don't know a whole lot about raising children unless they grew up in a big family and had to help. For us, it's been trial and error. We muddle through the best we can. I'm sure we make mistakes, but as long as we show them how much we love them, I think they'll be okay."

"How many children do you have?" Kyla asked.

"Two," he said. "Emma, who is growing up way too fast, is six going on thirteen. McClain is a little over a year old now. The boy learned to run before he could walk, and he hasn't slowed down since. I'll have him in a saddle before too long." Hank's eyes sparkled when he spoke of his children. The man was completely in love with them.

Kyla's heart warmed. Hank gave her hope that not all children were as unfortunate as she'd been growing up. "How is it being the husband of a famous movie star?"

"I wouldn't change a thing. I've loved Sadie all my life. It just took us a while and coming home to remind us what we found in each other. Basically, we're like any married couple, only better. The honeymoon will never end."

"You're lucky."

"Yes, I am." He lifted his chin toward her. "What about you? Any idea what you're going to do next?"

She shook her head. "First, I need to purchase a computer so I can start my job hunt."

"What about going to work for a magazine or local newspaper?"

"Not interested," she said. "They only like to report the bad stuff. I've had enough negativity and bad stuff for a lifetime. I'm ready for a change."

"What news organizations or magazines have you written for? Maybe I've seen your work?"

Kyla's belly knotted. Normally, she had no problem spewing falsehoods. They were part of the job. She hated lying to this man who'd done so much to get her out of Afghanistan, and now offered to let her stay with his family. If he knew she was an assassin, he wouldn't let her anywhere near his wife and children. "Since I freelance, my work is all over the place, and yet, not easy to find." Not exactly a lie and vague enough.

"I'm surprised you didn't get out before the Taliban seized control of the airport in Kabul."

"I wasn't in Afghanistan when they took over." Now, it would get sticky. "How did Brotherhood Protectors get its start?"

Hank met her gaze and held it a little longer than necessary, making his point. He recognized that she'd changed the subject.

Kyla didn't squirm or back down. Talking about how she got into Afghanistan wasn't an option. The less she said, the better.

He gave an almost imperceptible nod. "I would've stayed in the Navy, but I was needed back home in Montana. My father and Sadie had challenges to overcome. I couldn't go back to the career I'd chosen. In the process of protecting Sadie from a stalker, I realized I could still be the person I was meant to be, use the hard-earned skills I'd acquired on active duty and help others. When I hung my shingle, word-of-mouth spread, and I discovered there were many people who needed help."

"Did it take long to build up the business?"

"No," he said. "I had work from the very beginning and not enough people to handle it."

"What did you do?"

He grinned. "I invited SEALs, Delta Force and other Special Operations warriors who'd separated from the military to come fill the needs. Our clients got the protection they needed, and our highly trained former military found work that utilized their skills."

"A win-win situation for everyone." Yeah, so she'd been an assassin. Maybe that's why she appreciated books and movies with happy endings where nobody died either from being shot, blown up or suicide. "So many of our military folks have difficulty adjusting to civilian life."

Hank's mouth pressed into a tight line. "They think the only way out is suicide."

Kyla knew the statistics. "Thank you for giving them a better option."

Hank reached out and touched Kyla's arm. "I feel

like there's a lot more to you than we see on the surface."

She stiffened. Had she let her guard down too much?

"Don't worry." He gave her a crooked grin. "I won't pry. But if you ever need someone to talk to, you can always call me. I'll listen."

Her heart filled with something she hadn't felt in a long time...the warmth of human kindness. She'd seen the worst of the worst in people. Hank's genuine offer to listen meant more than she could ever express. "Thanks."

"I'm serious. You can tell me anything. If you want me to keep it to myself, I will. Sometimes, you have to let go of what's eating at you to fully recover from trauma." His eyes narrowed. "I sense you've had your share of trauma in your past. You don't know me well, but you can trust me with anything."

No, she couldn't. Not because he couldn't keep a secret, but because she didn't want to slip down in this man's estimation. And slip she would. He was good and kind.

She was a killer.

His brow furrowed. "Everyone has something in their past they regret. We're not perfect. I've done things I wish I could undo. I've killed people and caught innocents as collateral damage. I can't bring them back to life. All I can do is live my life the best way I can."

For the first time since she was ten and placed in

the foster system, Kyla's eyes stung and welled with tears.

She turned away from Hank and blinked them back, refusing to let them spill down her face. One escaped, and she quickly brushed it aside.

One of the reasons they'd recruited her into the team of assassins was her ability to maintain a poker face in all situations. Her hand-to-hand combat skills, marksmanship and her lack of a family had made her perfect for the job.

Had she gone soft? Tears were for the weak.

Another slipped down her cheek. Kyla let it fall, refusing to acknowledge its presence by raising a hand to wipe it away.

When she had her emotions under control, she faced Hank with a tight smile. "Thank you, Hank. I'll keep your words in mind." Without waiting for his response, she pushed to her feet. "I'd better get back to my seat and catch a few more Zs. It should be morning when we arrive in Montana."

He nodded. "I think you'll like it there."

She gave him a genuine, if tight grin, barely holding it together. "I'm sure I will," she murmured.

As soon as she stepped past Hank, she reached up and brushed away the tears. She didn't have time to feel sad or to wallow in pity, lamenting the lousy childhood she'd endured and the normal life she'd never know.

For Kyla, the *real* world was a harsh environment where people were the threat. Many times, they were people who were supposed to care about you. That's why she'd hardened her heart and refused to get close to anyone.

Her gaze sought Stone, and the wall around her solid heart crumbled a little.

He was sitting up, his brow furrowed, his gaze searching.

For her.

When he found her, his frown lifted, and he smiled.

The walls crumbled a little more, exposing feelings she should never entertain. Feelings led to pain. Why torture herself? In the past, the people she'd cared about left. In this situation, she would have to leave. Eventually, the people who had attacked her in Kandahar would catch up with her. She couldn't be around Hank and his family when that happened. She would never forgive herself if something happened to that nice man, his wife or his little ones.

Her shoulders squared. All the more reason for her to find the ones responsible and beat them to the punch. If she could get to the bottom of the Ahmadi hit and her burn notice, she might be able to stop them from accomplishing their mission.

Someone was hiding a big secret. One they'd kill to keep. Kyla would find out what it was and who was calling the shots if it was the last thing she did. In the meantime, she refused to let anything awful happen to the people who'd risked their lives to help her.

# CHAPTER 7

STONE HAD SEEN the tears glistening on Kyla's cheeks before she'd brushed them away and wondered what had made her sad.

She'd been sitting with Hank for several minutes. Had he said something that upset her? Hank wouldn't have intentionally hurt her. He wasn't that kind of guy. Something must have struck a chord with Kyla to make her cry.

Stone wanted to know what it was. He wanted to know everything about the mysterious woman who'd stormed into his life less than twenty-four hours ago.

When she settled in the seat beside him, he could sense she didn't want to talk. He bit back the hundred questions spinning through his head and reached for her hand.

She let him take it in his and hold it until she fell asleep.

Kyla slept the rest of the flight.

Stone tried, but he was too wound up, worrying about the tears, his future and the futures of his men. He'd feel a lot better after he and Hank talked. If Hank decided he couldn't use his guys, Stone would be okay with the decision. He'd come up with another plan. At least a decision would have been made, and he could move to the next option.

He owed these guys his best effort. They'd given him theirs. Several times during the flight between Nova Scotia and Montana, Stone had gotten up with the intention of marching down the aisle of the plane to Hank's seat and starting the conversation.

Once, he'd walked by and Hank had nodded off, the dark circles beneath his eyes a testament to his lack of sleep.

Stone couldn't wake him.

Another time, he was awake, reading a newspaper and drinking a cup of coffee.

Stone slowed but kept going. He hated asking for another favor before the first favor had concluded. They'd come this far, they could wait until they made it to the ranch and had a chance to rest. He wanted Hank to be alert and receptive to his idea.

Stone stood for a while, stretching his legs at the galley while the flight attendant poured him a cup of coffee.

He thanked her and carried the cup back to his seat.

Kyla stirred. Her lashes fluttered but she didn't wake.

Two cups of coffee and four magazines later, the flight attendant turned on the lights and passed through the cabin offering a breakfast of warm ham and egg croissants.

"Where are we?" Kyla whispered as her eyes opened and she stretched in her seat.

"We're less than an hour out of Bozeman," Stone said.

"Oh, good. I'm ready to have my feet back on the ground."

"How can you be so anxious about flying?" Stone shook his head. "You must've had to do it a lot in your line of work."

Her eyes widened, and she stiffened for a brief moment. Then she relaxed and smiled. "Yes. I did. And no matter how many times I tried to tell myself it's just a giant bus in the air, I still got wound up. If I can travel somewhere in a car, train or boat, I'd do it over flying any day. Unfortunately, some of those options aren't always available or feasible." She shrugged. "So, I grin and bear it and get on the damned plane."

He dipped his head. "I'm glad it didn't stop you from doing what you wanted to do."

"Or what I had to do," she added. "It's a necessary evil I deal with grudgingly." Kyla pressed the button on the side of her seat, sat up and deployed her tray table.

Stone had just extended his when the flight attendant brought their trays with steaming croissants.

"Much better than MREs," Dax commented from the seat in front of Stone. "But it's not a hamburger."

"Hold that thought," Hank called out. "Tonight. Blue Moon Tavern. You'll have it."

They ate quickly then helped the attendant police the cabin of the trays, empty water bottles and coffee cups.

By the time she'd stowed the last bag of trash, the captain came on, asking them to stow their tray tables and buckle their seatbelts for the landing.

Kyla reached for his hand this time and gave him a weak smile. "I know I shouldn't get used to this, but...whatever. You don't seem to mind, and it helps."

He curled his fingers around hers. "I don't mind at all." In fact, he was getting to where he liked holding her hand a little too much.

He suspected that when they were on the ground, he might not get the opportunity again. Aside from flying, Kyla seemed like she could handle anything thrown her way without falling apart. She wouldn't need to lean on anyone.

That made him wish the flight would last a little longer. Then again, the sooner they were at the ranch, the sooner he'd approach Hank with his proposal.

The pilot brought the plane down so smoothly, it kissed the runway with barely a bump. The reverse thrusters engaged, slowing them to a manageable speed to taxi. The plane rolled to a full stop in front of the general aviation terminal.

Once the engines were shut down and the cabin was secure, the flight attendant opened the door, lowering the steps to the ground.

Hank was first out of his seat and through the door.

His team and Stone's filed out.

Stone let Kyla pass in front of him, and then followed her down the aisles and out of the plane. When she reached the ground, a smile spread across her face, and she raised her face to the rising sun. She tipped her head toward Stone and whispered, "I'd kiss the ground, but that might be an insult to the flight crew. And they did an exceptional job."

Stone chuckled. "I've done it before after a particularly harrowing mission where our helicopter had taken fire. We didn't expect it to make it back to the forward operating base. When we limped in, a few nuts and bolts short, every man, including the pilot, dropped to the ground and kissed the dirt." He rubbed his chin.

"I can practically taste it," Kyla said. "I'll pass this time."

Three large black SUVs drove out onto the tarmac and parked close to the plane. Each had the words White Oak Ranch written in white lettering on the front doors.

The men stood on the tarmac, stretching their legs and backs, hesitant to get into the vehicles.

"We're not there, yet," Hank said. "Another forty

minutes, and you can relax and get your land legs back."

"We might need to do a little shopping while we're here in Bozeman," Bubba suggested, tugging at the flight suit that fit tightly on his big frame. "These monkey suits were fine for the long flight, but we could use some real clothes if we plan to go out for hamburgers tonight."

Hank's lips pressed together. "You're right. Bozeman is your only chance to get what you need. Eagle Rock doesn't have much in the way of clothing to offer." He nodded. "It's still early, but I think I can call in some favors and get some stores opened early for us. My team won't need to shop. They can continue on to Eagle Rock without us."

Kujo saluted Hank. "Thanks. I'd like to kiss my wife and baby hello."

"Me, too," Boomer said with a smile. "They'll be glad we got home so quickly."

"I might just have time to have breakfast at the diner before Lana has to go to work. Let's do this," Trevor said and led the way to the first SUV.

After the Eagle Rock team left, Hank climbed into the next SUV, his cellphone pressed to his ear, already working the latest challenge—getting a store that would meet their needs to open early.

Stone and Kyla rode with Hank and Dax.

The others crowded into the last vehicle, anxious to get what they needed and get on the road.

By the time they pulled up to a department store,

a man was unlocking the door just for them. "Come in. Come in. It might take a few minutes to get the computers up and running, but you can be looking around while I work the technology."

"I'll see you guys at the checkout counter," Kyla said and headed for the ladies' clothing.

Stone felt a strange sense of loss as Kyla walked away. Since he'd met her, they'd been together except when they'd showered at the airport.

As she disappeared into the rows of clothing racks, he wondered if this would be how he felt when she went on to her next assignment or job.

"Don't take all day," Hank called out to the men. "I have a wife and two kids waiting for me."

"Lucky bastard," Stone said with a grin.

"I know." Hank nodded toward a stack of blue jeans. "Need help finding a size?"

Stone shook his head. "Won't take me long." He looked around, searching for Kyla one last time.

"I'll keep an eye on her while you're getting outfitted," Hank said.

"I'm sure she'll be fine on her own." Stone frowned.

"Agreed, but something's off about her."

Stone nodded. "Not in a crazy way, but in a way that makes me think she might be in danger."

Hank nodded. "Has she said anything about her work in Afghanistan?"

Stone shook his head. "Not much. She—"

"—changes the subject," Hank finished. "Like I said...I'll keep an eye on her while you're shopping."

"You don't think she'll bug out, do you?" Stone asked.

Hank's brow furrowed. "I really don't know. If she does, she won't be your problem anymore."

"Yeah," he muttered, his gaze on the woman with the dark hair, looking out of place while wearing a military flight suit in a civilian department store. He didn't mind Kyla being his problem. As long as he knew where she was and that she was all right.

"Go on. I've got this," Hank said and followed Kyla at a distance.

Stone quickly selected a couple pairs of jeans in his usual size, a long-sleeve, white button-up shirt, a blue chambray shirt and a couple of black T-shirts, socks and boxer briefs.

His black combat boots would suffice for now. When he knew where he would land, he would send for the rest of the clothes he'd packed into the two suitcases that he'd left with a friend in DC after he'd let the lease on his apartment run out.

Purchases in hand, he headed for the checkout counter where the store manager waited for them to finish shopping.

He had the man ring up his items and paid for them with his credit card. After the manager bagged his items and thanked him, Stone went in search of Hank and Kyla.

He found Hank but saw no sign of Kyla.

Hank grinned and tipped his head toward a fitting room. "She had a handful of items. She might be a while."

"Why can't women shop like men?"

Hank laughed. "I've asked Sadie that on many occasions as I've held her purse while she tried on thirty outfits until she finally decided she didn't like any of them." His smile lingered. "Women are built and wired differently than men."

"No shit," Stone said.

"But they're amazing. Sadie might be a Hollywood sweetheart, but she can string barbed wire without shredding her skin, fix the hinge on a gate, haul hay and ride a horse like nobody's business. After a long day in the field, she'll jump in the shower, do her hair and makeup and dress like the movie star she is and remind you what it's like to be a red-blooded male. Then she'll gather her babies and rock them to sleep, singing so sweetly you'd think you'd died and gone to heaven where the angels live. Smart, strong, gentle and beautiful...all in one package." He shook his head. "That's a woman for you."

Stone studied his friend's face as his old battle buddy spoke of his wife. He envied Hank's life. The former SEAL had done it right by leaving the military and coming home to Montana. Here, he could be home more than gone. He could be there to watch his children grow and help his wife raise them to be good people like their mom and dad.

A movement caught his attention.

Kyla stepped out of the dressing room, wearing a pair of black jeans and a sky-blue sweater that hugged her body like a second skin, emphasizing every curve with grace and beauty. She carried a stack of other clothing items and the flight suit.

When she spotted them, she smiled. "I'll be ready as soon as I pay for these." She hurried to the counter where the manager was busy ringing up Moe's items.

None of the men had chosen to walk out in any of their purchases.

Kyla was last to pay. She had the manager cut the tags off the shirt and jeans she wore after she'd paid for them. She still wore the same boots she'd shown up in, but she had added a pair of high-heeled sandals to her purchases.

Stone had only seen Kyla in black pants and a black shirt or the baggy flight suit. The thought of her wearing the strappy heels made his groin tighten.

Dressed in more feminine clothing, Kyla appeared softer and more approachable. Had he imagined that "offness" about her? Her simple clothing transformation made her look like the girl next door.

Well, almost.

He'd never lived next to a woman as casually sexy as Kyla. Hell, she'd managed to look sexy in the baggy flight suit.

Oh, hell, he really had to get his shit together or he'd be falling for the woman. And that would be a mistake. Especially since he knew so little about her and she wasn't volunteering to tell him more.

# CHAPTER 8

KYLA PAID with a gift credit card she'd loaded with enough money to get her around while on assignment. With a smile, she thanked the manager for allowing them to shop before store hours. It felt good to have a few more clothes than what she'd worn when she'd left Kandahar. Too often she'd had to leave articles of clothing behind. Like she'd told Stone, she traveled light. Sometimes, too light. Someday it would be nice to have a closet in a house of her own where she could collect a few outfits that fit and looked good. She might even consider keeping more than one pair of boots, if she had a place to store them. She was tired of being a nomad.

The manager bagged her items and carried them around the counter. "If you're finished, I'll have to unlock the door for you to get out."

Hank glanced around at each man and Kyla. "Have what you need?"

Everyone nodded.

"Very well," the manager said. "Follow me." He led the way to the exit, unlocked the door and held it open. Hank was the last man out. He held out his hand to the manager. "I owe you one, Tom."

The man shook his head. "You've already paid with your service to our country. It's the least I could do to show my appreciation to each of you." He placed his hand over his heart. "Thank you for your service."

Hank shook the man's hand. "Thank you for your support. Come out to the ranch some time. We'd love to show you around."

Tom nodded. "I'd love that."

As they walked out to the SUVs, Bubba said, "If it's all right by you, we'd like to make a quick stop at a convenience store for junk food and sodas."

"Yeah," Dax said. "Now, you're talking."

"I'm in," Kyla said, Bubba's plea for junk food, making her smile. She could use a sweet fix and maybe some potato chips to munch on.

They piled into the vehicles with their packages and drove to the nearest convenience store. Kyla laughed at the childish delight the men displayed over the aisles full of snacks and the refrigerators full of chilled sodas.

They made their selections, paid and walked out of the store with their arms loaded with everything from carbonated beverages to potato chips and candy bars.

Even Stone came out with his own stash of his favorite caramel-filled chocolate bar and a sixteen-ounce plastic bottle of soda.

Kyla had snagged a small can of mixed nuts and a bottle of cranberry juice. It was enough and would hit the spot if she got hungry late in the night and didn't feel like wandering through a strange house in search of sustenance.

Back in the vehicles, they finally reached the road headed east out of Bozeman toward the Crazy Mountains.

Since Hank had one of his ranch hands at the wheel, he was free to point out landmarks and give a little of the history of some of the buildings and mountains along the way. The forty-minute drive passed quickly for Kyla as she sipped her drink and ate a couple of handfuls of nuts.

She couldn't help comparing the dichotomy of traveling the roads of Montana and the streets of Kandahar. She'd been running for her life not long ago. Today, she sat in a luxury SUV with a handsome man at her side, who made her heartbeat erratic, not out of fear, but most likely lust. With a mouthful of salted nuts in her mouth, she stared out at the Montana landscape that appeared so peaceful it was surreal.

The differences in her two lives hammered home the fact she was done with her old job. She wouldn't go back, even after she got to the root of recent events and cleared her name off someone's hit list.

The SUVs slowed as they entered a small town.

"This is the thriving metropolis of Eagle Rock," Hank said. "Don't blink, you might miss it. It's not much, but we like it here. We have a grocery store for most necessities, but if you want a bigger selection, you have to make the drive into Bozeman. We do have a diner and the Blue Moose Tavern where locals go to hang out, drink and get a decent meal with their beer. It's the highlight of most residents' week. And ours, too. We'll be here tonight for Dax's hamburgers."

"I look forward to it," Dax said.

Not long after they'd entered Eagle Rock, they were leaving.

Kyla grinned. "It's cute."

"We like it," Hank said. "Not all people are cut out for it though. Everyone knows everyone else's business. Except for the celebrities and big business CEOs who buy up huge properties and visit one or two weeks out of the year. Between them and the preppers hiding in the Crazy Mountains, and our usual natives, things stay interesting."

Kyla laughed. "What you're saying is it's not always as peaceful and idyllic as it looks."

"Exactly." Hank shot a glance back at Stone. "Keeps us in business."

Stone nodded. "Speaking of business..."

Hank grinned. "I was beginning to wonder if you'd ever get around to it."

Stone tensed beside Kyla. "I didn't want to bring

up anything new until our mission was complete. It didn't seem right to start something in the middle of finishing something else."

Hank chuckled. "That's how it works around here. There's always something happening, cropping up, finishing out, starting over…" He touched a hand to his chest. "It keeps us on our toes and the blood pumping."

Stone snorted. "No time to get old, huh?"

"Damn right," Hank said.

"I'd like to discuss a proposal with you when we get to the ranch and settle in."

"You're in luck," Hank said. "We're here."

The SUV turned off the main highway at a grand stone gate with an arched wrought iron sign over the top that read White Oak Ranch.

The driver leaned out and entered a code on the keypad. A moment later, the gate slid open.

Both SUVs pulled through, and the gate closed behind them.

"We have security cameras on the gate and the drive up to the house, as well as strategically located around the house and outbuildings."

"I can imagine Sadie's popularity comes at the price of your privacy," Stone said.

Hank nodded. "We do the best we can with the latest technology, and she never goes anywhere by herself. If I'm not with her, one of our team members is. Two, if she's in LA or on one of her shoots."

Kyla cringed at the thought of being in the public

eye all the time. She'd been successful as an assassin because she'd kept to the shadows, blended into the crowds and kept her head down.

Sadie McClain was everything Kyla wasn't—blond, beautiful, talented and gregarious. What the hell would they have to talk about? She could already imagine awkward silences stretching between them. She really should have left the men in Bozeman and moved on.

Stone reached for her hand and gave it a gentle squeeze. "We're here," he whispered.

The SUV emerged from the tree-lined drive into an opening where a house stood perched on a slight rise. The two-story structure with its rock and cedar exterior blended well with the backdrop of the Crazy Mountains and stands of lodgepole pine trees. It wasn't the garishly glamourous home of a movie star, but the home was stunning, with giant windows overlooking the surrounding mountains and forests.

As the SUV pulled to a stop in front of the house, Hank turned with a smile. "Welcome to our home."

The front door burst open, and a little girl with long, bright blond hair ran out onto the porch. "Daddy!"

Hank hopped out of the SUV and hurried forward, his arms open wide.

The child barreled toward him and leaped into his arms, wrapping her legs around his waist.

Hank hugged her tightly to him. "Hey, baby girl. Did you miss me?"

"I did," she said and leaned back to look into his face. "I'm glad you're home. We made cupcakes for you and your friends." She looked past him as Kyla, Stone and Dax climbed out of the SUV. The second vehicle pulled up beside the first.

Moe, Hunter and Carter got out, carrying their bags of clothes.

Moe whistled. "Dang, Hank. How does a person afford a place like this? Business must be really good."

Hank laughed. "I can't take credit for it. The property belongs to Sadie and her brother Ian. When the old home burned to the ground, she and I had this house built in its place. Come in. I want you to meet Sadie. She's the most amazing woman." He smiled down at the little girl in his arms. "This is Emma, the little girl who made me a father and changed my life forever." He kissed his daughter's nose. "I love you, Em."

His daughter blushed as every gaze was on her. "Daddy, don't. You're making me shy."

"Sorry, sweetheart. I just tell it like it is. You're my favorite daughter." He climbed the front porch stairs and opened the door.

"I'm you're only daughter." She shook her head, her blue eyes dancing.

Hank paused on the threshold. "Sadie! I'm home!" He passed through and waved the others to enter.

A stunning blonde crossed a massive living room, carrying a toddler on one hip. Her hair was a pretty mess, and her face flushed a glowing pink. "I'm sorry.

I was trying to get to you, but McClain had other ideas. I had to chase him down and practically sit on him until he let me pick him up."

The little boy reached his arms up to his father. "Daddy!"

Hank lowered his daughter to the ground and reached for his son. "Have you been terrorizing your mother?"

"No," baby McClain responded, all innocence.

Hank laughed and tossed the boy into the air.

The child giggled all the way up and back down. "'Gain," he demanded.

Hank tossed him up in the air again and caught him in a big hug.

"'Gain, Daddy," the boy said.

"Can't," Hank said. "I need to hug Mommy."

With McClain on one arm, Hank pulled Sadie into the circle of his other arm and kissed her soundly in front of everyone.

Seeing the family together, and the way Hank unabashedly demonstrated his love for them, made Kyla's heart constrict. This was what a family should look like. It was the kind of family she'd had before her parents had died.

That strong stab of envy twisted in her belly. Growing up in the foster care system, all Kyla ever wanted was roots, a family to love and to love her. Her throat tightened and her eyes stung, but she held it together a little longer.

When Hank finally raised his head, Sadie pushed

the hair back from her forehead. "Hank, we have company."

Hank looked over his shoulder. "And so, we do. Sorry, folks, you'll have to find your own bride...or groom to kiss."

Sadie frowned at her husband, tempering it with a smile tugging at the corners of her lips. "Hank."

"Right." He turned and introduced each of the men on Stone's team and Stone. When he turned to Kyla, Sadie smiled broadly.

"Sadie, this was our bonus prize from our extraction mission in Afghanistan. Kyla Russell, my wife, Sadie McClain."

Sadie held out her hand and gave Kyla one of her million-dollar smiles. "I'm so very glad to meet you. Come in." She hooked her hand through Kyla's elbow and led her through the living room into a bright and open kitchen full of shiny new appliances any chef would envy.

Sadie pulled a clear glass pitcher filled with pale yellow lemonade out of the refrigerator and laid it on the counter. "Would you like lemonade, wine or beer?"

"Lemonade would be lovely," Kyla said.

Everything about Sadie made Kyla smile. She made Kyla feel at home, like one of the family with just a smile and a touch of her hand.

"It's not quite noon, but I'll bet the guys will start in on the beer anyway." She reached into the commercial-size stainless steel refrigerator, pulled out a case of beer and set it on the counter.

As if on cue, Stone's team entered the kitchen, laughing.

Sadie welcomed them with a smile and waved them toward the beer and lemonade. "I know Hank will want to take you on the grand tour. So, if you want a drink to take with you, help yourself."

The men each grabbed a beer from the case and popped them open.

Sadie poured lemonade into two glasses and handed one to Hank along with a kiss. "Don't bore them for too long in your office. They might want to see some of the outbuildings and the sun setting on the mountains."

Hank pressed a kiss to Sadie's forehead. "Yes, ma'am. I promise to take good care of our guests." He looked around at the men, each holding an ice-cold beer. "Who would like to visit the heart of the Brotherhood Protectors?"

Every man raised a hand.

Kyla raised her hand along with them. She wasn't one of them, but she really wanted to see what kind of setup Hank had built into his private residence. "Do you mind if I come?" she asked.

"Not at all." Hank grinned and led them back through the kitchen to stand in front of a wall with what appeared to be a keypad.

Hank pressed his thumb to the pad and held it there for several seconds. A click sounded, and a door opened in the wall, revealing a staircase, leading into a basement. Hank started down. As he descended the stairs, motion-activated sensors went off, lighting the staircase until he reached the bottom.

Kyla wasn't much on the casual conversation some of the men engaged in, but she was interested in whatever computer setup Hank might have. She was the second one down the steps.

As she arrived at the bottom, she was amazed at what she saw.

The room was bright and uncluttered, with a long conference table down the center and an equally long whiteboard on one wall. In one corner stood an array of computer monitors mounted on the wall. Beneath the array sat a big man with a shock of white-blond hair.

"Gentlemen...Ms. Russell," Hank waved a hand toward the man in the corner, "this is Swede. He's in charge of everything pertaining to technology. Brotherhood Protectors could not do what it does without Swede's computer savvy, knowledge of various systems, support and dedication."

"Hey." Swede stood and held out his hand to Kyla first.

Kyla almost missed the hand, her gaze sweeping over the computers. When she realized he was waiting, heat rose up to her neck and into her cheeks. She grabbed his hand and gave it a brief but firm shake. "Are you on satellite or ground internet?" she asked.

Swede grinned. "Both, to ensure a proper backup."

"Smart," Kyla said and sank into awkward silence.

"While we have your team cornered and trapped in our subterranean hide-out," Hank said with a grin, "what is it you wanted to talk about?"

Stone frowned. "It might be better to wait until we can be alone."

"I have a feeling that what you want to talk about is as important to these men as it is to you." Hank clapped his hands together. "Gentlemen, please. Have a seat at the table."

Kyla remained where she was, looking over Swede's shoulder, pretending to ignore the group at the table, afraid that if they remembered she was there, they'd ask her to leave.

"Have a seat," Swede whispered, pulling up another office chair beside a keyboard. "We can watch the show from here."

She sat, angling her chair to the side as she would if Swede was showing her something on the computer. It gave her enough of a view of the men at the table and a clear line of sight to Stone.

He pulled out a chair, waited for his guys to take their seats and then sat in his. "First of all, I'd like to thank you on behalf of myself and my team for all you did to get them out of Afghanistan."

Stone's men raised fists in the air and shouted, "Hear! Hear!"

Hank gave a brief nod. "You're welcome. But I might have had some ulterior motives in rescuing your men." He held Stone's gaze. "But go on."

"Now that we're out of the Middle East, we're looking to start over Stateside and hope to connect with a security firm with a good reputation and strong leader." Stone's lips quirked upward.

Hank laughed. "Nice job of stroking the ego. Go on."

Stone nodded. "I'd like to bring my team of experts into the Brotherhood Protectors' fold."

Hank clapped his hands together. "Okay."

Stone frowned. "Okay?"

Hank nodded. "Okay. You're all hired."

# CHAPTER 9

THE MEN at the table all smiled at Hank's announcement. Stone was no exception. But his smile left his face sooner than the others. "I had one other part to that proposal."

Hank held up a finger. "Hold that thought. I want to hire your team, but you have to be willing to set up shop somewhere else. We have enough guys here in Montana for now. I looked into alternative sites and think I found one. It's not far from here, it does attract a significant number of people to the area and it has some potential training sites we can tap into for a special project I have brewing in the back of my mind."

Stone's brow furrowed. "The location of my team was the other idea I was going to propose."

"Great." Hank crossed his arms over his chest again. "As long as it's Yellowstone, we're in good shape." He cocked an eyebrow. "What site were you considering as a base for the new division of the Brotherhood Protectors?"

Stone shook his head, his mouth twisting into a crooked grin, his heart lighter than it had been in a long time. "You looked into my background, didn't you?"

Hank nodded. "I did. Your father has a lodge in Yellowstone, with a barn he doesn't use behind it. I think it would be a great location for the next branch of the Brotherhood Protectors." His eyes narrowed. "But why join us? Why not continue the Stone Security Agency? You had it built up nicely before the drawdown in the Middle East."

"I thought about that. And I would've continued the business, if things didn't pan out here. I don't want these guys left hanging. And I have more who might come back to us when we have the work for them. They'll be happy to be working Stateside."

Hank frowned. "Not all of our jobs are Stateside."

Stone glanced around at his men. "We expect that. But for the most part, we can put down some roots, if not in Yellowstone then in Eagle Rock or anywhere else there's a branch of the Brotherhood Protectors. A bigger organization provides more opportunities to share expertise, like Swede."

"Hey, leave me out of this discussion," Swede said. "I'm just the computer geek."

"Exactly," Stone said. "We had to wing it on our own, each doing his best to tap into the internet and databases to get the information we needed. None of us are really good at it." Stone glanced around at his team. "Am I right?"

They nodded.

Stone continued. "We can muddle through but would greatly benefit from having someone we could go to for help."

"I get that," Hank said. "Without Swede, we'd be sunk."

"Nah, you'd manage," Swede said, "but you'd struggle. I've seen you on a keyboard. It's not pretty."

Hank grinned. "Can't type to save my life."

Swede held up a hand. "I can attest to that."

"I've got enough on my plate here in Montana," Hank said. "If we set up shop in West Yellowstone, are you willing to head that division and keep the guys busy?"

Stone's face split in a grin. "Yes, sir."

"Good." Hank clapped his hands together. "The next question is when can you start?"

"Is tomorrow soon enough?" Stone shot back.

"You don't need any downtime? Time to visit your families or to spend on a beach full of bikini-clad babes?" Hank cocked an eyebrow.

"I don't need a break. I'm ready to get this party started." Stone turned to his team. "But if you guys want to take some time to decompress or visit family, now's the time to do it."

"Some of us will need time to move personal items out of storage and get our lives in order for a relocation to West Yellowstone," Bubba said.

"I'd like to find a lake or river to camp near and do some fishing," Hunter said.

Moe nodded. "Same."

"There are lots of good streams and rivers here in Montana or near Yellowstone," Hank said. "No one wants a beach vacation?"

"No way," Dax said. "I've seen and eaten enough sand to last a lifetime. I'm glad to be back in the States."

Hank nodded. "It'll take some time to transform the barn into your headquarters. I took the liberty of speaking with your father. He has a list of local contractors who could start right away on the work."

Stone shook his head. "When did you do all this?"

"I had Swede do a background check on you. I already knew your skills and moral integrity from our missions together, I wanted to see if you'd be interested in working with us, and if you had any other ties that might keep you from relocating to one of our current branches."

"Then why did you suggest a new branch in Yellowstone?"

Hank grinned. "I like the location. I think it has potential." His gaze traveled around the table. "Okay, then. Welcome aboard! Sadie has rooms set aside for you here at the ranch. Some of you will have to double up or sleep on the couch."

"Anything will be an improvement over the cold hard dirt floor of that cave," Hunter said.

"Or the cold hard, dirt floor of a Taliban prison cell," Moe reminded them.

"Yeah," Bubba nodded toward Hank. "Thanks for getting us out. We were running out of options."

"My pleasure," Hank said. "We'll celebrate freedom and new opportunities tonight at the Blue Moose Tavern. Now, if you'll excuse me, I'd like to go play with Emma and McClain before they go down for their naps. Feel free to look around our head-quarters, the ranch house and outbuildings. If you have any questions, ask Swede." Hank left them and climbed the stairs up to the main level of the house.

Once Hank was out of the room, the men looked around the room at each other and burst into grins.

"Yellowstone, huh?" Carter nodded. "I've never been, but I've seen pictures. It looks like an amazing place."

Dax's brow wrinkled. "Isn't that whole area considered a supervolcano?"

Stone nodded. "It was the site of several large eruptions, thus the name supervolcano."

"Should we be afraid of another anytime soon?" Moe asked.

"Who knows?" Stone said with a shrug. "It's been over six hundred thousand years since the last major eruption."

"What about smaller eruptions?" Dax asked.

"The last smaller one was more than thirteen thousand years ago." Stone shook his head. "I'd be more afraid of the Taliban invading the US than an eruption in our lifetime."

Moe sighed. "That's too bad. I've always wanted to see an active volcano."

"Well, you'll get to see volcanic activity in Yellowstone National Park," Stone said. "Old Faithful is a geothermal vent, releasing heat from the core. There are some hot springs you can soak in near the park as well."

Dax slapped a hand on the table. "That's what I'll do after I get my stuff moved from the storage unit in San Diego. Warm, wet and relaxing. That's more my speed. Right now, I want to get out of this monkey suit into some real clothes and explore Hank's place." He pushed to his feet.

"Sounds good. Maybe we can rustle up some chow for lunch. Is it too soon for that hamburger at the tavern?"

"That's tonight," Carter said. "I'm looking forward to good food, good beer and good company."

"It's a small town, Romeo," Bubba said. "You'll probably be stuck with us."

"Damn." Carter shook his head. "So much for good company."

All six men stood and headed for the stairs.

Stone hung back, turning toward Kyla. "Coming?"

She shook her head. "I have some questions for Swede. I'll be up after a while."

Still, he hesitated. He didn't want to leave her, even for a few minutes. Which was ridiculous. She was with Swede in a safe location. Nothing would happen to her. And she wouldn't disappear. Damn, he was getting used to having her around. "Okay."

KYLA WANTED to go with Stone, but she had work to do. When he finally turned and climbed the stairs to the top, she let go of the breath she'd been holding.

The entire time the team had been in the room, she'd watched as they'd interacted and poked fun at each other.

Kyla's heart swelled at the easy camaraderie of the team of men. They respected and trusted one another. She hadn't found that kind of connection in the CIA and never in her secret life as an assassin.

The men were lucky to have each other and a network of brothers who had their backs.

Stone had made a good point about joining forces with the Brotherhood Protectors to capitalize on shared expertise. Especially when it came to computers and the internet.

Kyla knew computers and how to get around on the internet. And she was fairly good at hacking into databases. At the very least, she knew people who were even better at it.

Her time in the CIA and on the Dark Web had paid off more than once. Ahmadi wouldn't have made it out of his home alive, if not for her contacts and her ability to ferret out the truth. She hoped it paid off in her search for answers to what had happened in Kandahar.

She needed access to the internet. Her gaze went to the computers, keyboards and monitors in the room. If she could use them while she was there, she might get a good start on her search for the truth.

When Kyla faced Swede, the big, blond man cocked an eyebrow. "Something I should know about you and Stone?"

Heat rushed into her cheeks. "Of course not."

"Sure." He turned toward the monitors and clicked a few keys, bringing up the security camera images. "What did you want to know?"

"I was hoping to conduct research on some of the people I interviewed while I was in Kandahar. Would it be possible for me to use one of your computers with access to the internet?"

Swede nodded. "I could set you up. I'll have to block your access to our proprietary data, but I don't see any problem with you using the internet."

She smiled. "I understand. I'm working on a story and need to pull together all the pieces."

Again, not a complete lie. She needed to know the full story in order to find those at the root of the kill order. No longer in Afghanistan, she couldn't just run out and ask people questions. All she could hope for was a trail of clues leading to the source.

Swede pulled a laptop from a shelf, spent a few minutes clicking keys until he finally handed over the laptop. "It's all yours. You don't have to stay down here if you don't want to. The WIFI works all over the house and out to the barn.

"If it's all right by you, I like the quiet down here. Do you mind if I stay?"

"Not at all. I'll be here for at least another two hours. I'm working on a project for Hank."

Kyla carried the computer to the conference table and sat facing Swede's back. If he turned around, he'd see her face, not her screen.

For the next two hours, she searched the internet for anything to do with illegal shipments of arms from the US to Afghanistan, US arms dealers suspected of illegal sales, politicians in bed with arms manufacturers and more. She sent a message to her connection in the CIA, asking if he'd heard anything about their agent Malik or his contact Ahmadi. Her contact said he hadn't, but he'd look into it and get back to her with anything he could find.

On the Dark Web, she put feelers out, asking for leads regarding the identity of Abaddon.

By the end of the two hours, she was discouraged and stiff.

Swede pushed back his chair and stood and stretched his arms, nearly touching the ceiling. "I'm heading up to find some lunch." The man was big and blond like a conquering Viking.

At a stopping point, code for hitting a wall, she was ready for a break and a chance to stretch her legs. "I'll join you."

As they walked to the top of the stairs, Swede asked, "Making any progress on your story?"

She shook her head. "Not really. I have feelers out, but there are too many gaps for me to get to the real meat of the issue."

"Anything I can do to help?" he asked.

"I'm not sure." She had kept her search to herself, afraid that if she shared anything about her flight from Kandahar, someone would figure out why she'd been there in the first place. But then, she could have been a journalist there to interview individuals for a story.

From everything Hank had said about Swede, he had to be good at what he did for the Brotherhood Protectors. He might be able to find information she wouldn't have considered. "Have you ever heard the name Abaddon?"

Swede nodded. "Hebrew for destruction. Why?"

She chewed on her lip for a moment before making a decision. "I was interviewing a man in Kandahar, who said a man going by the name of Abaddon was responsible for coordinating arms sales to the Taliban."

"So?" Swede pushed the door open and stepped out, holding it for Kyla. "I'm sure there are plenty of countries willing to sell arms to the Taliban."

"Including the US?"

Swede's jaw tightened. "I wouldn't be surprised. Though it would be illegal arms sales, if that's happening."

Kyla paused and considered her next words before voicing them. "I have it from a reliable source that the man I interviewed was targeted for elimination. Actually, I was with him when the attempt was made."

Swede shut the door to the basement and faced her. "Do you know who targeted him?"

Her mouth formed a hard line. "Someone in the US government."

"Why didn't you say anything when we first found you?" a voice said from behind her.

Kyla spun to face Stone.

His jaw was tight, his eyes narrowed. It wasn't the expression of a happy man.

Her face heated, and her palms grew clammy. "I didn't want to say anything at the time because I wasn't sure who I could trust." And she still didn't.

"Is that why you were in the back of the produce truck?" Stone asked. "You were running from the people who attacked your informant?"

She nodded. "When the attackers invaded my informant's home, I was the last one out. They saw me and came after me. I had to get out of Kandahar. It was night. They were dressed in dark clothing and ski masks. I couldn't even hide in the city, not knowing who they were. So, I ran."

Hank appeared from the direction of the kitchen. "Sadie made soup, and I made sandwiches for anyone who's hungry."

Stone stood still. His gaze locked with Kyla's.

"Maybe you should start from the beginning and tell us the whole truth."

Kyla's heart thumped against the wall of her chest. She wanted to tell him the whole truth, but she couldn't. What she could tell him was enough.

Enough for him and his team to understand what she was up against.

Kyla nodded. "Okay."

"Seems I've walked in on a serious conversation," Hank said. "Can we take it to the table, or is it private?"

She lifted her chin and stared straight into Stone's eyes. "We can discuss it at the table." She turned and followed Hank into the kitchen where the others had gathered around the table there.

"Sadie isn't going to join us," Hank said. "She ate with Emma and McClain and is laying down with them to try and get them to take a nap." He waved toward the table that had been set with plates, silverware and platters of sandwiches. In the middle was a large tureen filled with a hearty beef stew.

The men waited as Hank held a chair for Kyla.

After she took her seat, the others hurriedly claimed a chair and reached for the platters.

After everyone had a sandwich and a bowl of the soup in front of them, Stone nodded toward Kyla. "Our bonus rescue has more information she'd like to share about her escape from Afghanistan."

Kyla swallowed the bite she'd just taken from a chicken salad sandwich and placed the sandwich on her plate. "I wasn't just trying to get away from the Taliban. I was running from people who were trying to kill me and the same man I'd been tasked to...interview."

She told them everything that had happened, leaving out the part about her assignment to kill Ahmadi. When she was done, she looked around the table at the men who'd been so kind to her and had kept her safe from the Taliban.

She felt bad that she'd lied to them. In another world, she might have told them she was an assassin for the US government. But not this one. When she'd taken the job, they'd done a thorough investigation into her background and awarded her a super top-secret clearance, and had made her swear that she would take the secret of her job and assignments to her grave.

Even if someone in her own organization had gone rogue, or someone was pulling the strings even higher up, it didn't release her from her promise.

Or did it?

For a long moment after she stopped talking, no one said a word.

Then Bubba cocked an eyebrow. "Are you finished?"

Kyla nodded.

"Could you pass that platter of sandwiches?" he asked with a grin.

His comment got the rest of the men talking

again and reaching for more of the tasty chicken sandwiches.

"Unless one of the men following you actually saw you get into the back of that produce truck," Dax said between bites of his sandwich, "they don't know where you are."

"How could they?" Dax agreed. "We left on a plane that never landed in Afghanistan, from a landing strip without cameras or witnesses who could get close enough to see who got onto the plane."

"And she was dressed like a man, so she could've been just another American sneaking out of the country under the cover of darkness."

"They might still be looking for you in Kandahar," Moe said.

"I doubt it," Hunter said. "I wonder if Ahmadi and his wife got out."

"I wondered, too," Kyla said. "I spent time on the internet looking for any information about him and the CIA agent he met with. For the moment, no news is good news."

"I wouldn't be so sure that your troubles are over," Hank said from the end of the table.

All eyes turned to the leader of the Brotherhood Protectors.

"Why not?" Dax asked.

"If someone in the US government sent people to snuff Ahmadi, they don't want him ratting on this Abaddon," Hank said. "Kyla met with Ahmadi. They have to assume he gave her information they would rather not get out. If they think she knows too much, they might come after her again."

"If they can find her," Bubba said. "They might assume she's still in Afghanistan."

"I doubt they could trace her here," Dax said. "They wouldn't know she'd come with us."

Hank shook his head. "Our flight in and back out of the country can't have gone completely unnoticed. If there is a bad egg in the CIA, or whatever organization was tasked to assassinate Ahmadi, that guy is still there. He probably has access to information about military movements in and around that area. He could find out about the unsanctioned detour that C-17 made." He rubbed his chin. "They could question the crews of the plane and the helicopter. They wouldn't know any better than to tell the truth about the female they'd airlifted out of the country."

Stone's gaze met Kyla's. "You're not out of the woods yet."

She nodded. "That's why I spent the last two hours on the computer, looking for any clue as to who might be behind the attempt to kill Ahmadi and who Abaddon is. I feel like identifying Abaddon is key. If he's not the government official calling the shots, he works for him and could tell us who we're looking for."

"Well, that settles it," Hank said.

Kyla turned to the man at the head of the table. "Settles what?"

Hank's glance went to Stone. "Guess you have

your first assignment as a member of the Brother-hood Protectors Yellowstone division."

Stone frowned. "And what is that?"

"Kyla needs to be protected from someone in the US government who doesn't want anyone to know who is dealing arms to the Taliban."

Kyla shook her head. "I don't need to be protect-ed," she said. "I can take care of myself."

"And who will cover your six?" Hank asked.

She'd never had someone cover her back. She'd always worked on her own. "I can protect myself," she insisted. "What I could use some help with is chasing down leads. I need a computer with access to the internet and time to follow those leads. And I can't stay here for long."

Hank and Stone both frowned in her direction.

"Why?" Hank demanded.

"If someone is after me and finds out I'm here, that will put you and your family in danger." She shook her head. "We can't risk that."

"It will take time for them to find you," Hank said. "And we have a pretty robust security system in place."

Kyla shook her head. "You're right. It'll take time for them to find me. But I don't know how much time. I'm leaving tomorrow, anyway. I won't risk you, your wife or your sweet children getting caught in the crossfire. I probably shouldn't have come here in the first place." She pushed back from the table and stood. "I really should leave now."

Hank shook his head and stood. "Nonsense. You're staying."

"And tomorrow, you'll come with us to Yellowstone." Stone stood and met her gaze with a hard one of his own.

"That would work out well." Hank grinned. "Especially since she's now become your assignment."

Kyla didn't like that Hank thought she was someone who needed looking after. But then, she hadn't shared the fact that she was highly trained in combat skills and self-defense.

"I can help you from here with the internet searches and database access," Swede said. "You can take the laptop I set you up with and conduct your own inquiries from anywhere with internet access."

"In the meantime," Hank said, "Stone and his team will make sure you get the time you need to find out who's behind the attacks and what they're trying to hide. We could do it all from here at the ranch."

"Not an option," Kyla said, shaking her head.

Stone crossed his arms over his chest and pinned her with his gaze. "Then you're coming with us to Yellowstone."

# CHAPTER 10

"I DON'T KNOW what's keeping them." Hank twirled his cowboy hat in his hand and glanced at his watch for the tenth time. "We should be leaving now. It's a good thing I called ahead and had them reserve the back room for us."

"My guys will get there soon. I'm sure they'll hold our tables for us," Stone said. He didn't mind that they would be late. If he had it his way, he wouldn't go into Eagle Rock at all. He'd stay at the ranch with Kyla and keep her from venturing out into public.

His team had been looking forward to going into town, and they wanted him with them to celebrate their escape and, now, their new jobs. Stone didn't want to disappoint them.

When he'd suggested Kyla should stay at the ranch, she'd insisted on coming along. Sadie had chimed in and added her desire for Kyla to go as well.

Outvoted, Stone had conceded and asked Hank if he had a gun he could carry.

Thankfully, Hank hadn't hesitated. Instead, he'd taken Stone back down to the basement and shown him the armory where he was given his choice of handguns and a shoulder holster he could wear under the leather jacket Hank also provided.

"Some of our Montana team and their gals are meeting us at the tavern." He looked across at Stone. "It will be a good opportunity to introduce you and your team to some of your counterparts."

"Will the men who helped in the rescue be there tonight?" Stone asked.

"Kujo and Boomer won't be," Hank said. "They wanted to spend time with their wives and kids. Trevor will be there with his gal Lana. Swede and his wife, who happens to be my sister Allie, will be there and so will Taz Davila and his wife, Hannah. They live out at the Brighter Days Rehabilitation Ranch." Hank glanced at his watch again. "I should go see how long they're going to be."

"Don't get your chaps in a twist, cowboy," Sadie called out from the other side of the living room. "We wanted to make sure your wait was worth it." She struck a pose in her denim dress and cowboy boots. With her bright blond hair bouncing around her shoulders and a smile that could light any room, Stone could see why her fans adored her.

And Hank was her biggest fan. He crossed the

floor and held out his hand to her. "Wow, babe. You look amazing."

"Thank you," she said and stood on her toes to plant a kiss on his lips. Before he could take her in his arms, she turned toward the hallway she'd emerged from. "I think you'll both agree the wait was worth it. Come out, Kyla."

A moment passed.

Stone crossed to stand with Hank and Sadie. "Is she okay?"

Sadie laughed. "She's better than okay, just a little shy in a dress."

When Kyla stepped out of the master bedroom and into the hallway, Stone's breath caught and held.

She wore an off-white, off-the-shoulder dress that hugged her breasts and narrow waist like a second skin then flared out in three layers of flounces, falling barely down to mid-thigh. Around her waist was a braided leather belt with a shiny, round brass buckle. Her dark hair swung straight and loose around her shoulders and was crowned with a straw cowboy hat.

"Kyla is almost the same size as I am. I even found a pair of cowboy boots in my closet that fit." Sadie clapped her hands. "Isn't she adorable?"

Kyla's mouth twisted, and she tugged at the hem of the dress. "I'm not sure adorable is my style, and this dress is really short."

Sadie laughed. "It came down almost to my knees when I bought it. I had a seamstress remove one of the flounces. I think it looks much better shorter. You look amazing."

Kyla gave Stone a crooked smile. "I'm Sadie's science experiment. She works miracles."

"She had a good place to start," Stone said. "She's right. You look amazing."

Her cheeks flushed a pretty pink, making Stone want to pull her into his arms and kiss the lipstick off her lips.

"You look really nice," Hank said.

"Thank you." Kyla squared her shoulders. "We should be going."

Hank nodded and led them out to his truck where he'd parked it in front of the house.

While Hank handed Sadie up into the front passenger seat, Stone opened the back door for Kyla.

As she brushed past him, he caught a wisp of a subtle perfume. His groin tightened automatically. He really wished he was staying at the ranch with Kyla and not just to keep her safe. Hell, she might not be safe with him. Not while he entertained sexy thoughts about her.

She stepped up into the truck, exposing a significant amount of the skin on her thigh.

Stone swallowed hard to keep from groaning and hurried around to the other side and got in. He stayed on his side of the bench seat, afraid that if he accidentally touched her bare skin, he'd embarrass himself with a boner he couldn't begin to hide.

What was wrong with him? He'd seen a woman's

naked thigh before. He wasn't a teenager out on his first date. Hell, he wasn't even on a date with Kyla. They were only riding together.

Hank drove off the ranch and onto the highway, pushing the speed limit to get to the tavern on time.

Kyla reached across the bench seat for Stone's hand and gave him a shy smile. "You clean up well, Mr. Jacobs."

"You do, too, Ms. Russell."

"I'm sorry," she whispered.

He frowned and stared across the bench at her. "Why?"

"Sorry I didn't give you the whole story," she said. "There are things you don't know about me…"

And he wanted to know everything.

"At least I know now," he said. "It helps to have an idea of what we're up against."

She nodded and looked away. "I'm not good at opening up to people. I've always had to solve my own problems. It wasn't easy for me to ask Swede for help."

He lifted her hand and pressed his lips against the backs of her knuckles. "I'm just disappointed you didn't ask me first."

She shrugged. "I thought I could handle it on my own, but I was wrong, and your point about sharing expertise hit home."

"And you needed Swede's expertise." Stone nodded. "I get that."

Hank drove into the little town of Eagle Rock,

tucked in a valley between the peaks of the Crazy Mountains and parked in front of the Blue Moose Tavern. The parking lot was full of trucks, SUVs and cars.

"This place appears to be where it's happening," Stone said as he opened his door and dropped to the ground.

Hank got out, grinning. "We don't have a lot of choices of places to dine around here. We're thankful for what we have, and the food and service are good."

Stone and Hank hurried around to the other side of the truck to help the ladies down, both of whom had already helped themselves to the ground.

Hank held out his arm, and Sadie hooked her hand through her husband's elbow and smiled up at him.

Stone offered his arm to Kyla.

She slipped her hand into the crook of his arm and let him lead her into the tavern behind Hank and Sadie.

Inside, the tavern was humming with the sounds of people talking and laughing. All the tables were full, and the wait staff was busy seeing to customer needs.

Hank and Sadie wove through the tables to the back of the tavern and through a door into a private room.

As they entered, a cheer rose from the occupants.

Stone and Kyla stepped through the door to find

the room filled with people, some sitting, others standing, all talking at once.

Hank raised a hand, and the room went silent. "Just want to make some quick introductions, and then we can get to the business of ordering." He turned to Stone. "I'd like to welcome Stone Jacobs to the Brotherhood Protectors."

A roar of applause filled the room. When it died down, Hank continued to explain how Stone would head up a new branch of the agency to be based out of the Yellowstone area.

He went around the room, introducing the members of Stone's team who would go with him to the town of West Yellowstone, and then introduced the members of the Montana protectors who'd managed to come on short notice.

He started with a man with dark hair and dark eyes and a hint of a Hispanic accent. "Alex Davila, who prefers to go by Taz, and his lovely wife, Hannah. Hannah is a physical therapist working with veterans at the Brighter Days Rehab Ranch." Hank didn't give them time to shake hands with everyone but worked his way quickly through the people who were strangers to Stone.

"You know Trevor from the extraction mission. His lovely date is Lana Connolly. She works with Homeland security. There's always something interesting going on with them."

Hank pointed across the room. "And you know

Swede. With him is his wife, my little sister, Allie." Allie lifted a hand in greeting.

Hank turned around. "Did I get everyone?"

"You missed us," a voice called out from the door to the room. A man with brown hair and blue eyes entered with a woman with black hair and brown eyes, wearing a khaki-colored shirt dress and black heels.

Hank smiled at the latecomers. "Folks, meet Fin McClain, Sadie's brother, and his date, Aria Savage. I hope you all have a chance to get to know each other. Now, let's eat."

Everyone settled around the table, talking at once. Two waitresses worked the table, taking orders and delivering drinks and food.

Stone and Kyla sat close to Hank and Sadie. Throughout the meal, Stone talked with Hank about his plans for the barn and how he'd transform it into a modern office with the equipment necessary to run operations for their group.

"We really need to hire another Swede," Hank said. "He can't continue to do all the computer work for the organization. We've already farmed out the hardware maintenance and servicing. But we need people who can do what he does, digging into data-bases and running background checks on people."

Across the table, Swede nodded. "I love my job, but I can't be there 24/7. He tipped his head toward Kyla. "Our bonus rescue has some skills. I can imagine, as a journalist, you have to do a lot of investigative work to get your facts straight."

"I can get around," Kyla admitted, "but I'm not an expert."

"I can train the right person," Swede insisted. "Someone who has a knack for finding stuff."

Kyla laughed. "Based on my lack of progress today, that wouldn't be me."

"Swede's right," Stone said. "We could use a computer person in each of our offices." He wouldn't mind seeing Kyla's face every day. Then again, he'd rather see her face first thing in the morning on the pillow next to him.

Yes, he'd been angry that she hadn't told them the entire story about her daring escape from Kandahar and how she'd come to be in the little village.

Their meals were delivered, and the guys were delighted that the hamburgers were as good as Hank had advertised. Even Kyla ate one, fully loaded with all the condiments. She wasn't a woman who picked at her food, and she didn't have a spare ounce on her lean frame.

Stone wondered what kind of workout program she was on to maintain such great muscle tone.

After their plates were cleared, more drinks were ordered.

Sadie leaned across Hank and touched Kyla's arm. "Want to make a dash to the ladies' room with me?"

Kyla nodded. "Sure."

Stone and Hank stood and helped them to their feet.

As the two women left the private room and walked across the bar room, Stone watched from the door as they moved between the tables, heading for the hallway on the other side of the bar.

"Will they be all right?" Stone asked Hank.

"Weeknights are usually pretty quiet. Most of the rowdy patrons wait for the weekend to get drunk. But we can watch from here and step in if they run into trouble."

With the knowledge that someone wanted to kill Kyla ruminating in the back of his mind, he couldn't relax. Stone would rather have followed them all the way to the door of the ladies' room, but he stayed put and counted the minutes until the women reappeared, his gut knotting the longer they took.

# CHAPTER 11

KYLA HAD NEVER BEEN one of those girls who had to have a sidekick to go with her to the ladies' room. But she didn't mind playing sidekick to Sadie McClain. In fact, she was glad to go with her and make sure she wasn't accosted by a drunk or overzealous fan.

Sadie had been the consummate hostess, going above and beyond to make Kyla feel welcome and comfortable in her home. She'd insisted on loaning Kyla the dress she was wearing and had helped her apply a little makeup to enhance her eyes and lips.

For the first time in Kyla's life, she felt feminine and pretty. Not nearly as beautiful as Sadie, but maybe pretty enough for a certain former Navy SEAL to notice her.

And he had, his eyes lighting up when she'd stepped into the hallway at Hank and Sadie's house. Though she'd been annoyed at how long it had taken to get ready, Kyla had to admit it had been worth it to see the expression on Stone's face.

The majority of families that had come to eat had left, and the patrons replacing them had come for the drinks and company. As Kyla and Sadie wove through the tables, a couple of the shaggy mountain men called out to them.

Sadie ignored them and kept moving.

Kyla glared at one man who muttered lewd comments and started to reach out and touch her naked thigh. She dodged to one side, avoiding the man's groping hands. Had he touched her, she probably would have wiped the floor with him, dress or no dress.

She didn't tolerate men who thought it was all right to force their unwanted attentions on a woman.

They made it through the gauntlet and into the ladies' room where they used the facilities, and then washed their hands.

Sadie dabbed lipstick on her mouth. Her gaze met Kyla's in the mirror. "I think Stone has a thing for you," she commented.

What were they? In high school?

She shook her head. "I doubt it. We barely know each other."

Sadie gave her a knowing smile. "You don't have to know each other very long for the chemistry to work, and I see chemistry all over the two of you." She capped her lipstick and slipped it into her purse. "I'm glad you're going with him to Yellowstone.

They need a female influence to keep them out of trouble."

Kyla nearly laughed. She'd never considered herself a girly-girl. Far from it. All her life, she'd been more athletic than feminine. But tonight, in Sadie's dress, she'd finally felt...soft and...girly.

She'd never expected it, but hell, she liked it. And just because she liked feeling girly didn't mean she couldn't kick ass if the need arose.

"Want some lipstick?" Sadie asked.

Kyla shook her head. "No, thank you."

"You really don't need it. With your coloring, you have enough natural pigment in your lips that you really don't need to wear lipstick. Now, lip gloss is always a good option." Sadie smiled. "You couldn't care less, am I right?"

The disappointment in Sadie's eyes made Kyla smile. "I never really thought about how I looked."

"You don't really have to. You have a natural beauty and wonderful cheekbones."

Kyla stared at her face in the mirror. What was she supposed to say? She wasn't used to compliments. "Thank you."

"We'd better get back to our men before they come looking for us." Sadie pushed through the swinging door and out into the hallway, right into the arms of the drunk who'd tried to reach for Kyla's thigh.

The man wrapped his arms around Sadie and wouldn't let her go. "Lookie what I found. Sss-Sadie

McClain, the rich movie star, slumming with the lowlife for a night. Come, give me a kiss, pretty Sadie."

"You need to let go of me," Sadie said in her calmest tone as she struggled to free herself of the man's clutches.

When he didn't let go, she fought against the meaty arm clamped at a diagonal across her chest. "Sir, let go, or I'll scream," she warned. "I don't want to hurt you."

In answer to her warning, he clamped his other hand over her mouth and laughed. "All I want is a little kiss."

"Let her go, sir," Kyla said. She'd rather not have to take the man down.

"Who's gonna make me?" he said and grabbed a handful of Sadie's hair dragging her head backward. "Just one lousy kiss. Is that too mussch to ask for?"

"Yes, it is." Sadie cocked her arm and slammed it into the man's gut.

He released his hold on her hair and doubled over. "Bitch," he bit out and lunged for Sadie.

Kyla stepped between the man and her new friend. "Let's go ask the bartender to call someone to come pick you up."

She gripped his arm and guided him toward the bar.

The man dragged his feet and came to a complete stop. "Ain't goin' anywhere until that rich, movie star bitch gives me a kiss." He tried to go around Kyla.

In a swift move, she stepped in his way, narrowing her eyes. "Touch her again, and I'll wipe the floor with you." Planting her hands on her hips, she refused to budge. "Now, apologize."

"It's okay," Sadie said from behind her. "Just let him go."

"Why should I apologize?" he demanded. "She hit me. Now, get outta my way." He reached out and shoved Kyla.

Kyla's anger went from controlled to full-on kick-ass, take-care-of-business mode. She grabbed the man's arm, yanked him forward, ducked low and flipped him over.

He landed hard on his back, taking several seconds to catch his breath. Then he sat up, his face turning red. "Why I oughta—"

Kyla planted her boot in his chest and shoved him back to the ground.

He grabbed her foot and took it with him, then swept her other leg out from under her.

She landed on her side, twisted and had his neck in a leglock before he knew what hit him

"Apologize, dirtbag," she said through clenched teeth.

He clawed at the leg clamping down on his throat.

Kyla eased up just enough for him to push air past his vocal cords.

"Sorry!" he gasped.

She clamped her legs together again, cutting off his air. "Now," Kyla said, "when I let you up, you will have the bartender call someone to come drive you home. Do you understand?" Again, she loosened her hold slightly.

"Yes," he wheezed.

Kyla released her hold and shoved him far enough away so that she could get her legs free.

A hand reached for hers and pulled her to her feet. "Are you all right?"

She looked up into Stone's troubled face. "I'm fine."

"Damn, Russell, you've got some skills," Dax said from the end of the hallway. "Where'd you learn that move?"

Ignoring his question, Kyla stood back while Bubba hauled the drunk to his feet and led him away from the women.

Kyla turned to Sadie, who now stood in the circle of Hank's arms. "Did he hurt you?"

The beauty shook her head. "No. I was more concerned about you." Her lips twitched. "I guess I didn't need to be. You were amazing the way you took that man down so fast."

"He shouldn't have touched you," Kyla said, her hands still balled into fists, adrenaline still pushing through her veins

"I should've been with you." Hank hugged his wife tighter.

"Don't be silly," Sadie said. "Kyla had my six. What do they teach in journalism school these days?"

ELLE JAMES

"As a woman," Kyla said, "it's always good to know basic self-defense skills."

"Right, because you never know when you'll have to put a man in a leglock to get him to behave." Moe shook his head, a smile tugging at his lips. "Remind me not to make a pass at you."

Kyla pressed her lips together. "Don't be an ass, and you won't have a problem."

Carter laughed and pressed a hand over his chest. "Words to live by."

Hank looked down into Sadie's eyes. "Should we call it a night?"

She nodded. "Yes. I want to kiss my babies goodnight."

Kyla's heart squeezed hard in her chest. Hank and Sadie had what Kyla had always longed for. Loving acceptance and support.

Kyla's gaze met Stone's. "I'm ready to leave if you are. Or I can ride with Sadie and Hank if you want to stay with your team."

"I'm ready to go," he said. "The guys have their own vehicle. They can find their way back." He turned to Bubba.

Before Stone could say a word, Bubba nodded. "I've got this. I'll be the designated driver for these boneheads."

Moe pounded Bubba on the back. "Thanks, man. I'll pull DD next time."

"Yeah, yeah." Bubba rolled his eyes.

"Come on," Carter said. "We have some beer to

consume. Bubba's driving."

Hank thanked the members of his Montana team for coming and the new members of the Yellowstone team for joining the Brotherhood Protectors. Then he paid the bill, gathered his wife in the circle of his arms and led her out of the tavern.

Outside, a sheriff's vehicle had parked in the middle of the parking lot, and the sheriff's deputy was loading the drunk into the back seat with help from a couple of cowboys.

Hank had to wait until the sheriff's vehicle left with his passenger before he could back out of his parking space.

On the drive back to the ranch, Hank held the steering wheel with one hand his wife's hand with the other.

Sadie chuckled. "That was a lot of excitement for a weeknight in Eagle Rock."

"As a movie star, do you get accosted like that very often?" Kyla asked.

The blonde sighed. "More often than I'd like."

"I would like it to be never," Hank said, his tone tight. "I should've been with you."

Sadie turned to her husband. "Sweetheart, we've been to the tavern more times than I can remember, and I've never been attacked going to the ladies' room. You can't be with me every second of the day. Besides, I had Kyla with me, and she was badass." She shot a smile over her shoulder at Kyla.

"No kidding," Hank said. "Where did you learn that move where you got the drunk in a leglock?"

Kyla glanced out the window and told another half-lie. "I took self-defense classes. In my line of work, you never know when you'll have to defend yourself." And she'd had self-defense training in the CIA and a more intense version after she'd been selected by the secret assassination group. She could have tightened her hold on the drunk and held on long enough the man could have died.

Kyla hadn't actually learned the move for self-defense; she'd learned it as another technique to kill a man without putting a bullet in him.

Wouldn't that be a conversation she could share over lemonade with Hank and Sadie?

No.

Another reason she couldn't get close to these good people. Keeping the lies straight would become a real burden.

Tomorrow. She'd leave tomorrow.

If she were smart, she'd leave alone and start fresh somewhere else.

Stone reached across the bench seat and took her hand in his.

Why was it so hard to let go?

She stared at her hand in his.

Because she wanted to be with him so much, she would continue to make bad decisions.

. . .

STONE COULD FEEL the tension in Kyla. It had been there before they'd left for the tavern and had been amplified by the altercation with the drunk.

He wished he could take away some of the stress she was experiencing and make her feel better.

The only way to take away the stress was to help her identify the people responsible for placing the kill order on Ahmadi and then her.

He'd been serious about being less than helpful on the computer and internet.

Give him a gun and he could fight his way out of almost any situation. If researching the internet, the federal government and criminal databases would give them a lead to follow, he'd do whatever he could to help.

At the ranch, Hank and Sadie hurried into the house to check on their children.

Stone walked up the steps of the front porch with Kyla. When he opened the door, she didn't move through it.

"I'm not tired. I think I'll sit out here on the porch for a little while."

"I could use some fresh air." Stone closed the door and met her gaze. "Unless you want to be alone."

"I'd like the company, as long as it's just you." She turned away and leaned against the porch railing. "I don't usually go into crowded places if I don't have to." The muted yellow glow from the porch lights cast a soft light over Kyla, making her thick black hair shine.

Stone could not look away. "Then the tavern had to have been overwhelming. Being attacked must have been the last straw."

Kyla shrugged. "I kind of lost it there. The technique I used might've been a little more than was necessary to subdue the man."

"I think it worked perfectly," Stone said with a grin. "Have you ever had to use that move before?"

Again, she shrugged and didn't answer.

"I'm having a hard time figuring out just who you are, Kyla Russell. I pride myself on being a good judge of character. I think you're a good person, with a big heart." He turned her toward him and tipped her chin up. "At times, you're vulnerable, and yet, you can take a grown man down without breaking a sweat. What else should I know about you?"

She stared up into his eyes as if she wanted to say something. A moment passed, then another. She looked away and sighed. "If I told you everything there was to know about me, there would be no mystery." She gave him a weak smile. "And what's a woman without mystery?"

He shook his head. "I'm not buying it." He cupped her cheek and brushed his thumb across her skin. "Since you flung yourself out of that cave and into my life, I've wanted to know everything about you. What makes you laugh, what makes you cry, where you grew up, if you had pets, are you a dog person or a cat person? Who is Kyla Russell?"

Her gaze met his again, and her eyes shone with

moisture. "You don't want to know me," she said, her voice catching.

"Why?" He brushed his thumb across her cheek again. "Are you afraid of something? Are you married?" His brow furrowed. "You're not married, are you?"

She laughed. "No. I'm not marriage material."

"Why do you say that?"

Again, she looked away. "I'm just not."

"Because of what you do for a living?"

She looked back up, her eyes narrowing briefly. "Yes. It's hard to form any lasting relationships when you do what I do"

"But you said you were considering changing professions. You can build a new future."

She touched a hand to his chest and shifted her gaze to her fingertips. "Not if the past won't let you go," she whispered.

He tipped her chin up again. "We'll find the one responsible. Once he's locked up, you'll be free."

Her dark eyes, shadowed in mystery, stared up into his for a long, breathless moment. Then she leaned up and pressed her lips to his.

That brief touch sent a spark shooting throughout his body, igniting a flame that had been smoldering beneath the surface since he'd first held her hand while sitting beside her on the C-17.

As she withdrew, he pushed forward, wrapped his arm around her waist and crushed her to him, then bent to claim her lips in a kiss that rocked his very soul.

When her lips parted, he thrust past her teeth and swept the length of her tongue, tasting and caressing her until he was forced to come up for air.

His breath ragged, he leaned his forehead against hers and fought for control. His pulse pounded, and adrenaline rushed through his veins. He wanted more.

"Was that real?" she whispered.

"More real than anything I've ever experienced." Stone leaned back and stared down into her eyes.

"We don't know each other."

"And yet, I've wanted to do that practically since I met you." Stone shook his head. "I don't understand." He cupped the back of her head. "I've never felt that strongly drawn to anyone before I met you."

"Me either." Kyla covered his hand with hers. "Frankly, it scares the bejeezus out of me."

"Why?"

She shook her head and turned her face to press a kiss into the palm of his hand. "I'm no good at relationships. Any time I've ever dared to love people, they've died or left. I built my life around being alone."

"Is it what you really want? To be alone?" Stone asked.

She held his gaze for a long moment before answering. "No. But it's hard to change. Especially when you can't let go of your past."

"Have you tried?"

"Some things can't be overcome." Her lips curled into a sad smile.

"We all have our ghosts," Stone said. "You don't fight in wars without reliving so much of it in your dreams, wondering if you could've done better, or if you'd changed just one thing, would the outcome have been different."

"You're in a better place than I'll ever be," she said. "Don't settle for me. You deserve someone better."

His eyes crinkled, and a smile tipped his lips upward. "I'm not settling. I find you interesting, beautiful and strong. I want to spend more time with you."

She started to shake her head.

Stone captured her cheeks between his hands. "I'm not asking for you to commit. I'm asking you go with it, to take one day at a time. If the future makes you hesitate, stay with the present. Live each day, one at a time."

"Really," she insisted, her eyebrows forming a V over the bridge of her nose, "you should find someone without baggage."

"I like your baggage," he said with a smile. "I like the way you get all wound up on an airplane. I get to hold your hand and be brave for you."

She opened her mouth.

Stone held up a finger, touching it to her lips. "And I like that you can take care of yourself. Come with me to Yellowstone. Take it a day at a time. If what we're feeling now fades or doesn't work, we move on. At least we wouldn't look back and wonder if we'd made the wrong decision." He took her hands in his. "Yellowstone?"

Her fingers curled around his. For the longest moment, she didn't respond.

Had Stone read too much into her reactions to him?

Then her head lowered and came back up in a distinctive nod. "Yellowstone."

When his face broke out in a grin, she held up her hand. "Only until we figure out who was behind the attacks in Kandahar."

Stone tipped his head in agreement. "Deal."

It only felt natural to kiss on it. Stone lowered his head and brushed his lips across hers.

Her hands slipped across his chest and laced behind his head, bringing him closer. This time, she thrust past his teeth to slide her tongue along the length of his.

His body responded to her nearness. His groin tightened and he wrapped his arms around her, bringing her even closer. Her breasts pressed against his chest, warm and soft.

A groan rose up his throat. Stone broke off the kiss and drew in a steadying breath. "I can't."

"Why?"

"Because if I continue with this, I might not stop."

She smiled up at him. "So?"

He frowned. "I mean, I won't be able to stop at a kiss."

She blinked. Her smile spread, and her eyelids drooped. "So?"

"If you want me to stop, it has to be now." He shoved a hand through his hair. "Woman, do you have any idea what you're doing to me?"

She leaned into his hardened staff. "I have a good idea. You said to take it one day at a time. I'm taking it." Her eyebrow cocked. "Are you in?"

"Damn, Kyla." He looked into her eyes, his brow furrowing. "Are you sure? Once we start down this path, there's no going back."

She took his hand. "Then let me lead the way."

Stone had no choice. He was hooked and willing to let her reel him in.

# CHAPTER 12

THOUGH CONFIDENT IN her skills as an assassin, Kyla had never taken the lead in love-making. For that matter, she'd had long gaps between having sex. Mostly because she didn't feel the level of arousal that would make it worth the effort.

The amount of desire she felt for Stone was off the charts and consuming her like paper held to a flame. One kiss had set the flame racing through her veins, searing a path to her core. She didn't want the second kiss to end. It was the catalyst that awakened her senses to what could be if she let her guard down and lived in the moment.

Kyla led Stone through the living area.

Voices sounded from the kitchen.

Kyla slipped quietly past the kitchen door and headed straight for the stairs, hoping to avoid Hank and Sadie. She was glad the others had opted to stay longer at the tavern. Witnesses to their assignation made things messier.

She led him up the stairs and into the room Sadie had assigned to her. After Stone passed through the door, Kyla quickly closed it and twisted the lock.

Before she lost her confidence, she wrapped her arms around his neck, drew his head down and kissed him as if this would be the one and only time they would have together. As far as she was concerned, it had to be. She couldn't commit to more. Her past would eventually catch up to her and color her future, or worse. It could place Stone in danger.

However, at this moment, nothing mattered. Pushing her fears to the back of her mind, she lost herself in Stone.

As he returned the kiss, he walked her backward toward the bed.

Kyla slipped her hands between them and worked the buttons loose on his shirt from his neck to where it disappeared into the waistband of his jeans. Undeterred, she yanked his shirttail out and finished the job, pushing the garment over his shoulders.

He shrugged free of the sleeves, and the shirt fell to the floor.

With full access to his naked chest, Kyla ran her fingers across the warm skin covering rock-hard muscles.

Not satisfied to just touch him with her hands, she unbuckled the belt around her waist and draped the buckle over the end of the bed. Then she grabbed the dress's ruffled hem and dragged it slowly up her body, pausing along the way in hopes of increasing his desire and the sexual tension crackling in the air.

She laughed when he took over, yanked the dress the rest of the way off and slung it across the room with a growl.

"If you're going to tease," he said in a low, dangerous voice, "prepare to pay the price."

A shiver of anticipation rippled through her body. "Promises, promises," she said, daring him to make the next move.

His eyes narrowed, and his body tensed. He scooped her up in his arms and deposited her on the bed, pressing a kiss to her lips before he straightened again.

For a moment he stared down at her as if drinking in every detail of her body, now clothed in only a lacy bra and bikini panties.

Kyla held her breath, wondering if he liked what he saw, or if he found her lacking. She'd always considered her breasts too small and her shape too straight. Some women had narrow waists and more shapely hips. Not Kyla. She was slender and athletic. To her, that meant, boring.

The fire in Stone's eyes indicated he was anything but bored. He reached for the button on his jeans and flicked it open. As she'd done, he took his time lowering the zipper.

Once it was halfway down, his cock sprang free,

hard and straight.

Kyla's heart fluttered. She should have known he'd go commando. Now, she'd never look at his jeans the same way. She'd forever visualize that straining cock jutting free from the teeth of the zipper

Stone wasn't done yet. He hooked the waistband of his jeans and pushed them over his hips, easing them over his buttocks and then his thighs.

When Kyla couldn't wait another minute, she lunged off the bed, grabbed the waistband and dragged the jeans down to the floor.

Stone chuckled, kicked off his boots and stepped out of his jeans.

Kyla straightened in front of him, reached behind her back and flicked the catch on her bra.

Stone slipped his fingers beneath the straps and drew them over her arms, letting the bra drop to the floor.

He cupped her breasts in his palms and murmured. "Absolutely perfect."

She drew in a deep breath, her chest rising and falling.

Stone tweaked her nipples between his thumbs and forefingers, rolling them until they puckered into tight little beads.

Kyla's breathing grew ragged, and heat built at her core, spreading throughout her body. She wanted more. And soon.

Hooking her thumbs in the elastic of her panties,

she slid them over her hips and down to her ankles, stepping out of the last barrier between her and Stone.

She took his hand and backed onto the bed, scooting across to make room for him.

He laid down beside her and trailed a finger along her jawline, brushed his thumb over her lips and trailed his finger down the length of her neck. "You're beautiful," he said and followed the path of his finger with his lips.

Kyla had never considered herself beautiful. When Stone described her as such, in that tone, with that look...she believed.

Weaving her hand into his hair she urged him lower, eager to take things to the next level and the next one after that. Her body was on fire, and she wanted to burn with him.

Stone captured the tip of her breast in his mouth and sucked gently, flicking the nipple with the tip of his tongue.

Kyla's back arched off the bed, urging him to take more.

Instead, he abandoned that breast and moved to the other, rolling the tip between his teeth, while tweaking the first with his fingers.

Kyla moaned softly, her body tensing, ready, eager. Her hands moved through his hair and down over his naked back, alternating between smoothing, with her fingertips and digging in with her nails.

What he was doing with his tongue was pure magic. Still, she wanted more.

When he left her breasts, he skimmed his mouth across her ribs and downward, dipping his tongue into her belly button.

Finally, he reached the tuft of hair over her sex and rose up on his arms.

Kyla parted her legs, making room for his big body.

He settled between her thighs and blew a stream of warm air over her damp sex, igniting her nerve endings.

She shivered all over, waiting for him to…

With his thumbs, he parted her folds and scraped a finger over the nubbin between.

Kyla brought her knees up, dug her heels into the mattress and raised her hips, willing him to take more.

He touched her there with the tip of his tongue.

Kyla thought she would explode with the onslaught of sensations bursting through her. She was so close. All it would take was a little more—

Stone flicked her again, and she shot to the heavens like a firecracker, the fire starting at her core then expanding outward to the very edges of her being.

He continued flicking, licking and stroking her with that magical tongue while she rode the wave of her release all the way to the last pulsing quiver.

When she sank back to the mattress, breathing

hard and mostly sated, she knew it wasn't enough. Not until she had him inside her.

Digging her fingers into his hair, she tugged gently. "I. Want. You."

He chuckled and climbed up her body, stopping to claim her mouth with the taste of her release still on his lips.

His cock nudged her entrance—hot, hard and ready.

She gripped his buttocks and attempted to draw him in.

"Uh-uh," he said and kissed the tip of her nose. "Not yet."

"Yes. Yet," she argued, frowning.

He leaned away from her and reached for his jeans on the floor. Once he snagged them, he reeled them in and dug in the back pocket for his wallet. From inside the wallet, he extracted a condom.

Kyla heaved a sigh of relief. "I'm glad you're thinking for the both of us." All logic had left her head when Stone had kissed her. He, at least, was smart enough to remember protection.

The last thing she wanted to happen was to get pregnant She didn't know how long it would take to find the person who wanted her dead. She couldn't risk bringing a baby into the crossfire.

While he tore open the package, she reached down and wrapped her fingers around his thick shaft, curious to feel it wrapped in her fingers.

Curiouser still to feel it wrapped in her lips.

She pushed him over onto his back, grabbed the condom and set it aside on her empty pillow. Impatient to have him inside her, she wouldn't short-change him on foreplay.

After a long, hot kiss, she worked her way over his chest, flicking his skin with her tongue and kissing a path as she made her way down his body. She paused briefly to tap each of his little brown nipples with the tip of her tongue. Moving carefully, she turned her back to him, planted her knees on either side of his head and lowered herself over him.

His cock stood at attention, thick, hard and proud.

Kyla wrapped her hands around it and slid her fingers down to the base.

Stone bucked.

Kyla raised her hands all the way to the tip and back down again, pausing to fondle his balls. Cupping them in the palm of her hand, she touched the tip of his cock with her tongue.

It quivered, and Stone groaned. "You're killing me, Russell."

If only he knew that was exactly what she did. He might not be so eager for her to lie naked with him, holding his balls in her hands.

She flicked the tip of his cock again with her tongue and then took him into her mouth.

He thrust upward until he bumped against the back of her throat.

His hands gripped each cheek of her buttocks, his fingers digging into the flesh.

Kyla pulled back until her lips were at the rim around his head. For a long moment, she paused, milking his anticipation before she sank back down on him, taking him all the way into her mouth.

His hands clutched her ass, urging her lower until her sex hovered over his mouth.

He parted her folds and touched her there with his tongue.

She gasped and moved up his cock and back down again.

As he played her, she increased her speed, taking him in and out, again and again.

She teetered on the edge of another orgasm when he grabbed her hips, lifted her off of him and onto her back.

He came up on his knees, flipped her onto her stomach and raised her bottom. "Condom," he gritted out.

She reached for the packet that she'd left on pillow and handed it up behind her.

He tore it open, slid the protection over his cock and positioned himself at her entrance.

Kyla lay with her face on the pillow, her ass in the air, her channel slick and ready.

Stone didn't move.

"What's wrong?"

"I wanted to give you the chance to say no, but I'm

afraid you will." He laughed, his hands holding tightly to her hips.

"Oh, please, Stone," she begged. "Don't. Stop. Now."

That was all the encouragement he needed.

With his hands on her hips, he slid slowly into her, giving her body a chance to adjust to his thickness and her juices to lubricate his shaft.

"Oh, yes," Kyla moaned, burying her face in the pillow, afraid she might cry out loud enough to draw attention to her room. What she was feeling was so good it made her want to call out Stone's name and shout Hallelujah.

As he thrust into her, she rocked back, taking everything he had. Her fingers curled into the comforter as she held on for the ride.

Stone's speed increased until he was pumping in and out of her.

Kyla's breath caught and held, her body tensing, sensations pushing her to the very edge until she shot over, her release coming hot and fast.

Behind her, Stone's hands tightened on her hips. He thrust one last time and held her bottom pressed tightly against him. Inside her channel, his cock pulsed his release.

His hands slid up her sides as he leaned over her and cupped her breasts. Eventually, he slipped from her channel, stripped off the condom and folded it into a tissue, tossing it into the wastebasket.

Kyla collapsed onto her stomach, her body limp, her energy drained and herself completely satisfied. She lay with a smile on her face, the sheets brushing her naked skin causing little spasms at her nerve endings.

Stone lay down beside her and pulled her back against his front, spooning her. Skin to skin.

His cock was still hard and pressed against her buttocks.

If he gave her a few minutes, she might be up for round two.

"You know you're not a one-night stand," he whispered against her ear. "One night is not nearly enough."

She nestled against him, daring to dream they could have more than one night. Pushed to the back of her mind was the reality that it couldn't happen. Kyla wouldn't think about tomorrow. Not when she was living in the moment. Tomorrow was another day. Another moment. She'd deal with it then.

Tonight, she was with Stone. That was all she needed. Until her past came calling.

Stone lay for a long time, taking in everything about Kyla from the way her hair smelled to the curve of her earlobe. He wanted to wake up with her beside him every day…of his life. Though he'd only known her a short time, he felt connected to her in a way he couldn't imagine letting go.

He'd never believed in soul mates. Until now. Until Kyla.

And he felt as though he could lose her too

easily. Whether it was the assassins who'd attempted to kill her in Kandahar, or her own certainty that she was destined to be alone because of some misguided belief she wasn't cut out for relationships, their days together might be numbered.

He had to convince her that she needed to stay with him. If she was in danger, she couldn't leave alone. No one would have her back. She had to stay with him so he could keep her safe. He'd do everything in his power to help her find the answers she needed to stop those who were selling arms illegally and killing anyone who tried to stop them.

Tomorrow, they'd head for Yellowstone. Some of his team would be with him, and they could stay at his father's lodge. The lodge had internet. They could continue to search for clues and tap any resources she had as well as what Swede and Hank could come up with.

Hank had already contacted a security expert to install a state-of-the-art security system. They'd promised to put a rush on it and install it within the week.

Stone would rather wait at Hank's place until the security system was installed at the lodge, but he knew how worried Kyla would be. If they weren't going to leave for Yellowstone, she'd head into Bozeman and rent a hotel room until they were ready for them in Yellowstone.

No. That wasn't an option. He felt he could keep

track of her better in the small tourist town of Yellowstone than the larger city of Bozeman.

He was anxious to get to his hometown and dive into the barn renovation. They needed a base for their operations, an office where they could conduct their business, interview clients and former military for possible employment, and they needed a place they could gather to plan their missions.

The great room in the lodge would have to do until then. It wasn't private, and they couldn't store equipment there, but they could meet as a team in the space until the renovations were complete.

He knew he couldn't keep Kyla from leaving, but he could give her a job so that she felt productive and help the Brotherhood Protectors Yellowstone get their feet on the ground. She could help plan and organize the renovations in her spare time while she worked leads for her investigation.

Her focus would have to be on her investigation into the Kandahar incident. Only if she hit a wall and needed something to keep her busy would he draw her into the effort to set up the business.

On the other hand, if she helped, she might build a connection or bond with the new business and the team working it and want to stick around to ensure they'd succeed. And if she worked the business as support staff, Stone would see her every day. She wouldn't get too far out of his sight.

First hurdle was to get her to commit to going to Yellowstone and not a hotel.

Stone leaned into Kyla, closed his eyes and committed her scent to memory.

Whatever happened over the next few days or weeks, Stone had to stay on his toes and check-in with Hank and Swede daily for any updates on their efforts to help Kyla.

In the meantime, he needed to leave her bedroom to avoid being spotted by members of his team, Hank and Sadie. He wanted to keep what they'd done between himself and Kyla.

He considered her a work-in-progress. He liked her and wouldn't give up on her. Whatever ghosts she had lurking in her past would have to move over.

With a plan in his head and a beautiful woman spooned in his arms, Stone dared to be optimistic. So far, they'd seen no sign of any killers lurking in Eagle Rock. The sooner they left for Yellowstone, the sooner he could get started on convincing Kyla to stay forever.

# CHAPTER 13

A SOFT KNOCKING sound pulled Kyla from a dream where she'd been running and running, chased by men dressed in black clothing and black ski masks. They had been catching up to her. No matter how hard she'd run, she hadn't been able to outrun them.

When the knocking sounded again, Kyla sat up straight in bed. That's when she realized she was completely naked, and Stone had gone.

"Ms. Russell," a voice sounded on the other side of the door.

She couldn't make out who it was because he was obviously trying to keep the sound down to avoid waking the others.

"Just a minute," she called out. Kyla ran for the bag of clothes she'd purchased the previous day at the department store and dug out the jeans and a sweat-shirt and pulled them on.

Finger combing her hair, she hurried toward the

bedroom door, peeked through the little hole and shook her head. A giant of a man with pale blond hair stood on the other side of the door.

Kyla jerked the door open. "Swede? Why are you up so late?"

He chuckled and shook his head. "It's morning."

She frowned, still groggy from sleep. "Really?"

He shrugged. "Early morning, but the sun will be coming up soon. I got here early to work on your case and thought you might want to put in some time as well."

Stone planned to leave for Yellowstone fairly early. Once on the road, she'd be without internet capability to continue her search for at least a couple of hours. "Let me put on my boots, and I'll meet you downstairs."

"I'll be in the kitchen making coffee."

"Perfect," she said. Kyla closed the door and ran around the room collecting her things, stripping the sheets from the bed and pulling on her boots. She used the bathroom, washed her hands and face, brushed her teeth and hair and was finally ready, all in less than five minutes. She left the room, closing the door softly, and tiptoed down the stairs and into the kitchen.

The scent of freshly brewed coffee made her smile, and she reached for the cup Swede had just poured for her.

"Sugar or cream?" he asked.

"Black." Kyla wrapped her hands around the hot

mug and inhaled the steam rising from the dark brew.

"Black is the only way to drink coffee," Swede said.

"Agreed." She took one tentative sip, burned her tongue and met Swede's gaze. "Ready?"

He nodded and led the way to the bio scanner, entered the code and his thumbprint and the door opened.

They descended the stairs into the basement, the motion sensors triggering the lights to come on.

The laptop was where Kyla had left it the day before on the conference table. She booted the machine and waited for it to come alive.

Within minutes, she was in, checking her messages and surfing the internet for clues. As she'd done the day before, she checked for any news pertaining to Abdul Naser Ahmadi and Jalal Malik. Neither name popped up on the web.

For the moment, Kyla preferred to believe that all was well, and they'd found a place to lay low for a while.

She checked for messages from her contact in the CIA. At first, she didn't think she'd received anything. Just to make sure, she checked her spam folder and found a new message with a confusing subject line and an even more garbled body.

She was about to delete the message as spam when she noticed a pattern in the garbled text. Alphabetical letters had been interspersed with punctuation marks like asterisks, exclamation points and pound signs.

She wrote the letters on a pad, and her stomach sank.

When she stripped out the punctuation marks, she could read the message.

BEWARE OF A FOX IN OUR HENHOUSE. ABADDON LIVES.

"Swede?"

"Yes, ma'am." He looked across the floor from his computer. "Find something?"

"Maybe," she carried the laptop to him.

The upper door to the basement opened, and lights lit the staircase as Hank descended, followed by Stone, each carrying a steaming cup of coffee.

"You two are at it early," Hank said.

Stone's gaze locked with Kyla's.

For a moment, she forgot they weren't the only ones in the big room. Memories of the night before flooded through her mind, heating her soul.

Hank crossed the floor to where Kyla stood beside Swede, still holding her laptop. "Anything interesting turn up?"

"Kyla was about to show me something," Swede lifted his chin toward Kyla. "Whatcha got?"

Kyla pulled her gaze from Stone's and focused on the laptop screen. "Look at this."

The men studied the email.

Swede shook his head. "Either the email was compromised, or the system chewed up words."

"I stripped all the special characters out and got this." She laid the pad of paper on the desk beside the laptop.

Stone leaned over her shoulder to read the words. "What hen house?"

"I assume the US government," she said. And by US government, she suspected the CIA or the secret assassination group. The fox in the henhouse had to be the man who either called the shots or worked for the guy who called the shots.

"It's not much," she said. "Definitely not enough to find our guy, but it's a start and confirms that there's something going on in our government. My contact wouldn't send me an encoded message like this if he wasn't concerned."

Swede rubbed his chin. "Since your informant mentioned Abaddon, we can assume he's the one your Afghan interviewee told you about."

Hank frowned. "But who is Abaddon?"

Kyla shrugged. "I'm hitting walls. There isn't anything about him on the web." Kyla turned to Swede. "Any luck on your search?"

Swede shook his head. "I've been following news releases and bumping into bank accounts of our most likely arms dealers. It's slow work and requires further digging to chase the money trail through the weeds."

"Finding anything?" she asked.

He nodded. "Not enough on arms dealers, but I found interesting articles accusing Ethan Piker."

"Isn't he the guy who started Victory Tactical, the mercenaries for hire?" Stone asked. "He was kind of a competitor for my team."

"What do you mean kind of?" Hank asked.

Stone's lips pressed into a thin line. "Where we were providing security for contractors, he was providing armies for hire under the guise of a security firm. They staged raids into complexes controlled by the Taliban. Particularly, those locations the Taliban had seized control of that were of interest to US corporations."

"I read something about that," Hank said. "Didn't the Taliban get control of a precious minerals mining operation?"

Stone nodded. "Ethan Piker's mercenaries got it back and turned it over to the Afghan government."

"A lot of good that did, considering all of the country is now under Taliban control," Swede said.

"From what I'd read, Ethan made a pile of money on that raid. He couldn't care less that the Taliban eventually got it back. The Afghan government paid Piker."

Hank's eyes narrowed. "And the Afghan government got the money to pay them from the funds the US had been funneling into the reconstruction of the Afghan infrastructure."

"In other words, a few corporations benefited at the expense of taxpayer's money," Kyla said.

"Especially Piker's." Swede tapped his fingers across the keyboard and brought up information on

Ethan Piker. "The man has been lobbying with the US government to civilianize armies. He claims his organization can do what the American military can't."

"Never mind the people he hires are trained by the US military." Stone stared at the images on the array of monitors. "So, what does he have to do with Abaddon? Is he Abaddon, the man coordinating the sale of arms to the Taliban?"

Kyla had the same thought. The key piece of information Swede didn't have was that the US government had sent an assassin to kill Ahmadi. Someone higher up in the chain of command had made that call and authorized the kill.

"If Piker is lobbying the US government for civilianized armies, are there any government officials backing him?"

Swede bounced through screens of news articles, photographs of Ethan Piker meeting with foreign nationals, corporate CEOs and politicians. That might take more time.

Kyla nodded. "We need to find out if Piker has connections with arms dealers and any politicians. The hit on Ahmadi could've been hired out to mercenaries, or it could've been something the US government ordered."

Stone frowned. "Why would the US government assassinate one of their own spies?"

"How many elected officials get campaign funding from big business?" Kyla shot back.

Stone's mouth quirked upward on one side. "Too damn many."

"I'll keep looking," Swede promised.

"And so will I," Kyla said. "If I can have continued use of the laptop and internet…"

Hank nodded toward the laptop. "It's yours for the duration of this case. Swede will set you up with all the electronics you might need."

"Thank you, Hank," Kyla said. "I'll get back to work as soon as I'm set up in Yellowstone."

"Speaking of which," Stone said, "Hank's sending us down in two of his vehicles with weapons from his armory."

"That's right," Hank said. "That's why we came down here in the first place. The armory is over here." He led the way, and Stone followed.

Kyla closed the laptop. "Do you mind if I tag along?"

"Not at all."

Kyla caught up as they reached a door with a bio scanner and keypad on the far side of the room.

Hank entered a digital code and pressed his thumb to the scanner. The lock disengaged, and he pulled the door open.

Inside was an armory with a large variety of weapons, including AR15 semi-automatic rifles, specialized sniper rifles with long-range scopes, handguns of various calibers and even compound bows and smoke grenades.

"Take what you'll need to get started," Hank said.

"When you get the barn renovated with a controlled-access safe room, we'll stock it with the weaponry you'll need to conduct operations."

While Hank worked with Stone, discussing the attributes of each weapon, Kyla roamed the room, pausing in front of a specialized sniper rifle like one she'd been issued for a special assignment to take out a military leader in Ghana, who had been responsible for the torture and deaths of thousands of civilians, including women and children. That had been one of her assignments she'd been one hundred percent in agreement with. No one had suspected a woman of firing the shot that rid the country of a brutal tyrant. For that assignment, she'd hit the range for several weeks to become proficient with the weapon at multiple distances.

"Ever fired one of these?" Hank said from behind her.

She nodded.

"I'd like to have at least one sniper rifle," Stone said.

"Done." Hank pulled the rifle off the rack and stacked it with Stone's other selections. "I'll pack these up with boxes of ammo and load them into the SUVs you'll take to Yellowstone."

"Thanks," Stone said. "I'm anxious to get there and start working on setting up shop."

"I've already got a few contacts interested in our services in that area," Hank said. "I need to follow up and nail down the specifics. By the time your team is fully in place, we'll have work for them."

Hank turned to Kyla. "With the potential of you being a target, would you feel more comfortable armed?"

Her eyes widened. "You'd trust me with one of your weapons?"

Hank smiled. "I'm a good judge of character. It would be on loan, and I'll have you sign for it."

Shocked that he'd loan her a weapon, all she could do was nod. "Thanks."

Stone touched her arm. "We need to gather our team and hit the road. Are you ready?"

She nodded. "I'm packed. I just need to grab my bag."

Hank led the way up the stairs, carrying several of the rifles Stone had selected for his team.

Stone carried the sniper rifle and two other rifles slung over his shoulder as well as two handguns.

Kyla was loaded down with metal cases of ammunition.

Once they reached the top, Hunter, Moe, Carter and Dax hurried forward to help with their load.

"You'd think we were about to start a war," Dax said.

"Hopefully not," Hank said.

"We don't know what type of weapon will be necessary for each job," Stone explained. "I selected a variety to start with."

"We're really going to do this, aren't we?" A grin

spread across Moe's face. "I've always wanted to go to Yellowstone. And to think, we're going to be based out of there." His grin broadened. "Hot damn!"

Stone chuckled. "I hope you feel the same after winter. If everyone is ready, I'd like to get going. I have a lot to accomplish before dark."

They loaded their few belongings into the SUV and added the weapons and ammunition.

By ten o'clock, they were driving away from the White Oak Ranch, heading southeast for West Yellowstone, Montana.

When Stone climbed into the driver's seat, Kyla purposely claimed the seat behind him, allowing one of his men to ride shotgun. He was working now for Hank Patterson and the Brotherhood Protectors. He didn't need to spend time with her when he needed to work out details with his team.

The drive would only take two hours and they'd travel through some beautiful country surrounded by the towering peaks of the Rocky Mountain range.

After leaving the ranch, internet was basically nonexistent. Kyla settled back in her seat and drank in the beauty of the scenery around her.

Several times during the drive, she made eye contact with Stone via the rearview mirror. Each time, her body flamed, reminding her of the previous night she'd spent in his arms.

Her self-proclaimed promise never to commit to

any one person stood on shaky ground when she stared into Stone's blue eyes.

He made her want things she could never have.

STONE HAD BEEN DISAPPOINTED that Kyla had chosen to sit behind him instead of in the passenger seat where Bubba had taken up residence.

He wondered if she was mad that he hadn't stayed the entire night with her. When their gazes met in the rearview mirror, he sensed no animosity. However, he swore that he detected a flare of desire in the flash of her brown-black eyes.

Bubba and the guys kept the conversation going with their plans to visit Yellowstone National Park in the next day or so, hiking and maybe trying their hands at fly fishing in one of the mountain streams.

They asked about the setup at his father's lodge and where their headquarters would be. Stone assured them they would have a say in the design of the barn remodel.

His team had been through a lot and deserved a chance to have input into their home office.

Home office.

Home.

The closer they got to Yellowstone, the more excited Stone got. He hadn't come back often because it was hard to pack up and leave each time when his heart was in the Rockies.

He was like two different people: the hardened

warrior who would do anything for his brothers and the young man who'd grown up in the mountains and had always longed to return.

Ahead a plane moved into view, following the highway, heading their way.

"Is that a small plane in the distance?" Bubba asked

"Appears to be." Stone frowned, focusing on the aircraft. "Or an even smaller plane closer than we think...?"

Something left the body of the plane and shot toward them.

"Fuck!" Stone yelled. "Incoming!" He swung the steering wheel to the right as a missile whizzed past and hit the road where they had been a moment before.

The SUV swerved off the highway onto the shoulder and down into the ditch.

Stone drove several yards in the ditch then back up onto the pavement. "It's an armed drone," he said. "Warn the others."

"It's circling back," Kyla yelled from behind Stone.

He glanced in the rearview mirror.

Kyla swiveled in her seat, studying the sky behind them. She unbuckled her seatbelt and dove over the back of the seat.

"What the hell?" Stone struggled to stay on the road and watch what Kyla was doing at the same time.

Bubba was on his cellphone, trying to get a call to the SUV behind them.

The road curved around a hill.

Stone focused on driving. If the drone didn't pick them off, he didn't want to be the reason they died that day because he couldn't keep the vehicle on the road.

The road straightened, and they emerged on a long straight stretch in a valley. They'd be sitting ducks when the drone cleared the top of the hill and came back into their line of sight.

"Stop the car and open the hatch," Kyla yelled from the back.

"Are you crazy? That drone will nail us if we're sitting still."

"Stop the vehicle!" she yelled.

Stone jammed his foot on the brake, drove onto the shoulder of the road and brought the SUV to a halt. He punched the button on the dash to pop the hatch, then threw open his door and jumped out.

As the SUV behind them approached, he waved for them to keep going as he raced to the back of his vehicle. "Go! Go! Go!" he yelled to the driver.

Hunter hit the accelerator and shot forward as the drone topped the hill and came into sight.

Stone rounded the rear corner of the SUV and slid to a stop.

Kyla knelt on the ground, balancing her elbow on her knee, her cheek pressed to the side of the sniper rifle. She raised the barrel of the weapon, tracking the drone.

Stone held his breath as she did.

With an almost imperceptible movement, she caressed the trigger.

Bang! The bullet left the weapon.

A second later, the drone exploded in the air, pieces falling to the ground

"Holy shit!" Bubba shouted from the other side of the SUV.

"Whoop!" Dax yelled. "Did you see that?"

Bubba and Dax rounded the back of the SUV and stared, slack-jawed at Kyla as she lowered the sniper rifle and pushed to her feet.

"That was you?" Dax stared at Kyla. "You shot that drone out of the sky?"

Kyla didn't answer. Her gaze met Stone's.

"Damn, Stone. I thought you'd fired that shot," Bubba said, his tone one of awe.

"It wasn't me," Stone said, his tone even, his gaze unwavering. "It was our *journalist*."

# CHAPTER 14

KYLA PULLED BACK THE BOLT, expelled a live round and checked that the weapon was clear before she laid the rifle in the back of the SUV, avoiding eye-contact with Stone.

Kicking a drunk's ass in self-defense was one thing. Shooting a drone out of the sky using a long-range sniper rifle was another skill she couldn't explain away as easily.

"Wow," Bubba said. "Color me impressed."

"I don't think I could've done better," Dax said.

The other SUV turned around and drove back to where they had stopped.

Stone turned away from them and stared out over the valley to the side of the hill where the drone had gone down. "Think we can find the parts that might identify that drone?"

"Maybe if we stuck around for a day or two," Dax said. "It went down in that stand of trees."

Stone shook his head. "No. We need to move on. Someone knows where we are. If we stay here, they could come back with another drone or in vehicles." He turned back to the SUV. "Let's keep moving. When we get to an area with better cell service, we'll report the incident to the local sheriff's department and Homeland Security. I'm sure they'll want to follow up on someone firing missiles from a military-grade drone."

Bubba pulled out his cellphone. "Dropping a pin on this coordinate. I'll shoot it to Hank when we're in cell tower range."

The men climbed into the vehicles.

Kyla silently slipped into the back seat behind Stone. They were back on the road to Yellowstone, moving a little faster this time.

Kyla held her breath, praying no one would start asking questions about her drone kill-shot. Her prayers went unanswered when Dax turned to her, shaking his head. "Damn, Russell, where'd you learn to shoot like that?"

She looked up to find Stone staring back at her in the rearview mirror with narrowed eyes. She lifted her chin and met his gaze. "I've had training."

"What journalist school did you go to?" Dax asked.

"It wasn't a school for journalists, was it?" Stone said, his tone hard, his back ramrod straight.

Kyla shook her head.

"So, you're not a journalist." Dax's lips twisted.

"That makes more sense and explains why you were able to subdue that drunk so effectively last night."

"So, where did you get your training?" Bubba asked. "Military?"

She shook her head, not wanting to talk about it, but knowing she'd have to say something to satisfy these highly trained veterans.

"No more lies," Stone said. "Who do you work for?"

"When I swore in," she said. "I promised to never reveal that knowledge."

"It appears someone already knows," Stone said. "When you were with that Afghan, Ahmadi, in Kandahar—why were you there?"

"I'd rather not do this while you're driving," she said.

Stone snorted. "I'd rather not have missiles fired at me."

She held her tongue, refusing to talk until they were off the road and she could face him.

"Fine," he said. "We'll be there in twenty minutes. Then I want the whole truth."

She met his gaze in the mirror. "You'll have it."

For the rest of the trip, she sat silently, avoiding his gaze and rehearsing what she would say when they finally stopped and got out of the vehicles.

There was no good way to say what she had to. No way to make it sound any better.

She was an assassin. She'd killed people. When

she confessed to Stone her real career, it would change everything.

She shouldn't care, but she did. A long-term relationship with him wasn't possible. She'd known that from the beginning. She'd been recruited because she had no family, no ties, no one to hold her back.

For one night, she'd suspended reality and lived in the moment, daring to think she could have a different life. Reality had a way of slapping her in the face. Or sending missiles from drones to remind her that she was dangerous to be around.

She started to tell Stone to drop her off at the nearest truck stop, but she knew he wouldn't. At least, not until he got the full truth.

Then he'd want to be done with her.

She'd move on like she always had with everything she owned in a plastic trash bag.

A lump lodged in her throat, and her eyes stung. Since her parents had died, she'd held her feelings in check, refusing to cry when she'd been passed from foster home to foster home.

Why was she on the verge of falling apart now?

She raised her head, her eyes meeting Stone's again in the rearview mirror.

For the first time in her life, she'd let her guard down. She'd made the mistake of opening her heart, telling herself it was only for a night.

Ha. Not only had she lied to Stone, she'd lied to herself.

As they drove into West Yellowstone, she tensed.

The time of reckoning had come. She'd tell Stone everything she could. She wouldn't go into all her assignments, just the last one she'd failed. It was enough for him to know what she'd been, what she'd done. If he didn't ask her to leave, she'd have to decide then if she could stay long enough to find the answers she needed to stop whoever was behind targeting Ahmadi and her. Someone inside her own government was dirty. Before she walked away from her former job, she'd expose that person and make sure he was brought to justice. Having access to the internet and to Swede's expertise would make the search go faster. If she had to, though, she would move on and figure it out on her own.

Stone drove into West Yellowstone on North Canyon Street. The streets were lined with rustic stores, restaurants and T-shirt shops that catered to the over four-million visitors who came to Yellowstone National Park each year.

They turned right on Yellowstone Avenue and drove to the very western end of town. Stone pulled into the parking lot of the Grand Yellowstone Lodge. The three-story, rustic building wasn't quite what Kyla had expected. She'd thought Stone's father would have run a smaller, establishment with twenty rooms. This place probably had over a hundred. No wonder his father wanted him to move home and help with the family business.

Stone got out of the SUV and stood for a moment, staring at the building.

"Dude," Dax said, "is this where you grew up?"

Stone shook his head. "Not hardly. My father bought this place after I left for the Navy. It didn't look like this when he signed on the bottom line. It was a rundown mess. He's done a lot to breathe life back into it. I remember riding my bicycle past this building as a kid. It was rundown then."

Kyla stood back, putting distance between herself and Stone. This was his homecoming. His time to reflect on his past, his childhood and the memories this town invoked.

There would be time to come clean after they got settled in.

A man stepped out on the wide front porch. Probably in his late fifties, the man was broad-shouldered, with salt-and-pepper gray hair and piercing blue eyes. He looked like a finely aged version of the man who stood looking up at the lodge.

"Dad." Stone smiled, climbed the stairs and engulfed the man in a long, hard hug.

When the two broke apart, the older man's eyes glistened. "Son, welcome home."

Stone looked past his father to the lodge. "I can't get over the transformation. I don't remember this place ever looking this good."

His father's chest puffed out. "I tell you, son, it took a lot of sweat and money to bring it back up to its original glory."

"It's amazing." Stone turned to the members of his

team as they climbed the stairs to the porch. "Guys, this is my father, John Jacobs."

Bubba extended his hand. "Nice to meet you, Mr. Jacobs."

Stone's father shook Bubba's hand. "Call me John. We're not very formal around here."

"Yes, sir," Bubba said. "Stone told us you are prior military."

John stood taller, nodding. "Ten years in the Marine Corps. I left when my wife got sick and brought her and Stone out here when he was just a toddler." He nodded toward Stone. "He had to go and join the Navy to see the world."

"And now that I have, I'm back," Stone said.

"I'm glad, son. I've missed you."

"Same," Stone said.

John shook hands with the rest of the team and finally looked past them to where Kyla stood at the base of the steps. "I didn't realize you had a female member of your team," his father said.

"I'm not a member of the team." Kyla climbed the steps and shook Mr. Jacob's hand. "I'm kind of like a stray they kindly adopted."

"She's our mascot," Dax said. "And she's got some wicked moves."

Heat suffused Kyla's cheeks. Dax wasn't holding a grudge against her. "Nice to meet you, Mr. Jacobs. Your lodge is lovely."

"John," he said and held out his arm. "Let me show you around. I have rooms blocked at the back of the lodge with a view of the National Forest. And the barn, of course."

Kyla felt awkward taking John's arm. This homecoming was not about her. But she couldn't insult the man by ignoring his chivalry. She slipped her hand through the crook of his arm and let him lead her into the lodge.

He toured them through the lobby with the cathedral ceiling and a massive stone fireplace. Leather couches and chairs provided places for people to gather.

"I didn't do all this work myself. I had help from contractors, some old friends and veterans who needed work when I needed them to work. Between all of us, we got this place up and running. After all the construction and remodeling was finished, two of my buddies stayed on. I have a great staff to man the reception desk, wait tables and to keep the rooms and common areas clean."

Stone shook his head. "And here I thought you needed me back home to help run this place."

"I like to think this place could run itself." John gave his son a crooked smile. "I wanted you home for purely selfish reasons. I missed my only son."

Kyla's heart pinched hard in her chest. The love between the father and son was apparent and unabashed. Stone was lucky to have that kind of familial love.

John led them through a dining room and into a kitchen where a man with a shock of white hair stood in front of a stove, stirring the contents of a massive stockpot. He looked up and grinned. "Is this them?"

John nodded and waved a hand toward Stone. "Cookie, my son, Stone. Stone, Mike White, better known as Cookie, was once a chef aboard the USS Carl Vinson aircraft carrier. He helped serve over six thousand seamen daily. Now, he's serving our guests the best food in the state. He's the most important member of the staff here at Old Yellowstone Lodge."

"Ha," Cookie said. "We're fully aware that we wouldn't know how to turn on the lights without Tinker. But thanks." He wiped his hands on a towel and came around the stove to shake Stone's hand.

He shook hands with the other members of Stone's team, and then smiled when he got to Kyla. "And who's this pretty young thing?"

Kyla's face heated. "I'm Kyla," she said. "Nice to meet you." The more people she met, the worse she felt. They were good, hardworking people, and it was a waste of their time to get to know her when she wouldn't be around for long.

HE'D HAD at least half an hour to calm down after the drone attack and Kyla's demonstration of expert marksmanship. Stone was still angry and distrustful of her, but he couldn't help thinking that Kyla fit in with the rustic charm of the lodge.

The woman wasn't a girly girl. Though she'd been

a knockout in the dress she'd worn the night before, she seemed more comfortable in jeans.

"Any idea where we can find Tinker?" John asked Cookie.

Cookie tipped his head toward the rear of the building. "I think he stepped out to the barn. When Hank Patterson called and expressed interest in setting up shop here in West Yellowstone, he got all excited. The man needs a project. He's good for fixing things, but he's happiest remodeling and building things."

John chuckled. "I think he's measured every inch of the old barn at least ten times since the call. Come on, I'll show you what you'll have to work with. Just so you know, while the lodge is up to par, we haven't done much with the barn, other than clean it and put a fresh coat of paint on the exterior."

"That's fine. I'm sure Hank and I will have our own ideas about how to lay out the interior." His father seemed so much older than he'd been just five years ago when he'd visited Stone in San Diego. Why had he stayed away so long? He and his father had been tight when he was young. After his mother's death from pneumonia, they'd only had each other. His father had done everything to make his childhood happy.

John led them back through the dining room to the lobby and out through the back door. The rear of the lodge had a long porch like the front. In the yard beyond was a playground, a sand volleyball court and two horseshoe pits. A wide path led through a stand of trees to a barnyard with a huge old barn painted a dark red.

"I spend all my time on the lodge," John said. "I didn't have the time or the desire to revive the trail ride business the lodge used to have back in the 1970s."

"You had enough going on without adding to it." Stone wished he'd been there to help. From what his father had told him about the place, he'd gathered his old man loved the lodge, the people he worked with and his life in West Yellowstone.

John opened the big barn door wide and left it open. "Check it out. I think it will work for what you have in mind."

Stone stepped through the door into the huge barn. Old stalls lined each side. It was almost a shame to take the stalls out and replace them with office equipment, computers and a conference table. But then, they weren't going into the horse-riding business.

A man emerged from what once must have been the tack room, wiping his hand on a rag.

"Ah, Tinker, there you are," John said. "Come meet my son, Stone, and his friends."

Tinker joined them and shook hands with each person, one at a time.

"I've known Tinker, or Tim Smith to his mother, forever. He and I served together in the Marines. He was our unit's motor pool mechanic. Now, he's essential staff around here. As old as this place is, something's always breaking. Tinker can fix anything. In his spare time, he's rebuilding an old M1 Abrams tank."

Stone grinned. "What are you going to do with a tank?"

"What does any man do with a tank?" he countered.

Dax snorted. "Any damn thing he wants."

The men laughed and walked around the barn, talking about plans to transform it into usable office space.

All the while they talked and planned, Stone kept Kyla in his peripheral vision. She didn't join in the planning, keeping herself separated from the others, unlike the night before. A crease had taken up residence on her forehead.

Despite his distrust and disappointment at not getting the truth from her, he still wanted to reach out and smooth the frown from her brow. A journalist in a war-torn country had it hard. But she wasn't a journalist. If she was a secret agent, her work would have been even more challenging. A secret agent would have all the reasons not to tell him the truth and to concoct a plausible story. She'd have every right to keep all information to herself.

Still, he wanted the truth. If for no other reason than to keep her safe. If he didn't know the entire story, they might not be fully aware of what, or who, could harm her.

His father glanced at his watch. "Damn. I'm sorry, but I've got to bug out. I promised to help serve tables at lunch. One of our waitstaff had to take her child to the doctor. She's going to be late. Please, join us in the dining room for lunch!" He reached out and pulled Stone into his arms. "Thank you, son," he said.

"Thank me for what?" Stone asked.

"For making an old man happy. See the receptionist at the desk; she'll give you room keys. See you in the dining room," he said and hurried out of the barn.

Stone and his team stayed a few more minutes and then opted to get their gear and settle into their rooms.

They left the barn, passed through the lobby and out to where they'd parked the vehicles.

"We can wait to carry the guns up to our rooms until after dark. I don't want guests to think we're here to start a war."

Kyla retrieved her clothes bag and the computer case Swede had packed with the chargers she'd need.

Once they had their room keys, they bypassed the elevator, climbed the staircase to the second floor and walked to the back of the building where their rooms were located.

Kyla had the room beside Stone's. She slid her key card across the locking mechanism and pushed through the door.

Stone would have followed her in, but they weren't alone in the hallway. Instead, he entered his room and dropped his bag on the bed. Back out in the hallway, he tapped lightly on Kyla's door.

She opened it immediately and held it as he passed through into the room.

He wanted to pull her into his arms and kiss her long and hard.

Kyla stepped away, her back straight, her chin held high.

Her pride and determination made him want to grab her and shake her. To keep from doing that, he crossed his arms over his chest and looked down his nose at her. "Why?"

"Why did I lie?" She laughed with no humor. "The truth is nothing you would want to hear."

"Try me," he challenged.

Her lips pressed together for a moment before she spoke. "I didn't go to interview Ahmadi."

"I figured as much. Why did you go to his place in Kandahar?"

She looked away for a moment, and then drew in a breath and let it out. Kyla faced him, the shadows beneath her eyes more pronounced. "I went there to kill him."

# CHAPTER 15

"I'll need a little more than that," Stone said.

Though it went against her promise of silence when she'd gone to work for the super-secret assassination team, she had to tell him.

"I was an agent with the CIA when I was recruited to join a special projects organization specializing in assassination."

She paused, waiting for him to express his horror and disappointment. "The team is so secret there isn't a name for it and probably no written records. I didn't even know the name or face of my handler."

Stone frowned. "How did you receive assignments?"

Kyla pulled her cellphone from her pocket. "He would text me with instructions and a dossier on my target. I took that information and researched my target on my own."

"Why?"

"I wanted to know that the person I was going to kill deserved to die."

"And did they?"

She nodded. "Men known for torturing innocents, genocide and human trafficking. Some were politicians who did these things and got away with it."

"How did you feel about killing these strangers?"

She lifted her chin and met his gaze head-on. "How did you feel killing the enemy?"

He tipped his head. "Point made. What went wrong in Kandahar?"

Kyla looked away. "I researched Ahmadi. Nothing came up. He appeared clean."

"But you went to his place anyway," Stone said. "Why?"

"I watched him, thinking I might catch him doing something heinous." She shook her head. "He didn't. Except he met with a sleeper CIA operative. I touched bases with one of my old colleagues in the CIA who identified the agent. He was legit, and so was Ahmadi. I decided to ask Ahmadi why someone would want to kill him."

"And that's when he told you about Abaddon?"

She nodded. "While we were talking, men in black ski masks unloaded in front of Ahmadi's house. I helped him and his wife over the fence and told them to run. I hung back and led the attackers away from Ahmadi and his wife. At first, I thought the men in ski masks were after Ahmadi, but they were after me.

I think whoever put the hit out on Ahmadi hired the men in the ski masks to take me out after I finished my job. They never saw Ahmadi. Only me."

"Any other lies or omissions?" he asked.

"I can't tell you the names of my other targets," she said.

"I don't want to know."

"I'll understand if you want me to leave. I lied to all of you," she said. "Besides, it could be dangerous for anyone to be around me. I'd hate anyone to be collateral damage if someone comes after me."

"You're staying," Stone said.

"I can walk to a truck stop and catch a ride from there. You don't have to bother with me anymore." She grabbed her bag and the computer bag. "I would like to keep the computer a little longer. At least until I find out who is doing this."

"Did you hear me?" Stone gave her a lopsided smile. "You're staying."

She held her bag of clothes to her chest, feeling like the foster kid about to be moved to another home. "Why? You saw what happened with the drone. They could come again."

"Then we'll be ready." He took the bag of clothes from her hand and set it on the bed. "Bubba is reporting the drone incident. If they search for the parts, they might come up with a clue. Swede is still working to find connections. And he will. That's his expertise."

"I'll work on it, too, with the computer Hank

loaned me."

Stone nodded and repeated for the third time, "You're staying."

Kyla nodded. "But why?"

He closed the distance between them and cupped her cheek. "Because even when I'm so angry with you that I could explode, I still want to do this." Stone's mouth crashed down on hers, stealing away her breath.

She rested her hands on his chest, curling her fingers into his shirt. Being with Stone made her forget everything else and gave her hope for the things she never thought she could have.

When he ended the kiss, he stepped back. "I'll be back in a few minutes. I need to talk to Bubba and get on the phone with Swede and Hank."

"I'd like to be in on any conversation you have with them regarding this case," she said.

"Okay. And if you learn anything, in your research, I'd like to be clued in. We can't help you unless you share everything. The tiniest bit of information could be the key."

She nodded. "I know."

"I'm going to my room to call Hank now and let him know what you've told me. If they have anything new, I'll bring you in." He kissed her once more and backed to the door. "Rest. I'll be back in a few minutes."

He left, closing the door behind him.

Kyla touched her fingers to her warm lips and

closed her eyes. That had gone much better than she'd expected. He hadn't been horrified by her confession, and he hadn't packed her up and dropped her off at a bus station.

Instead, he'd kissed her and indicated that he and his team would continue to help her.

She walked toward the window and stood to one side of the actual opening. Her training had included not being visible in a window. She'd shot into upper windows on some of her assignments. It was important to be invisible.

Kyla stared out at the volleyball court and playground. The lodge would be a fun place to vacation with a family.

She wondered what it would be like to have a family with Stone. Their children would have dark hair and maybe blue eyes, like Stone's. She would want more than one child. Having been alone much of her life, she would never wish that for her child. If she decided to have children. If she could ever stop running from her past.

She stepped into the bathroom, washed her hands and splashed water on her face.

Her heart felt lighter. Stone hadn't asked her to leave. The problem was, they'd found her on the road to Yellowstone. They'd find her again.

She hurried across the room to the backpack and pulled out the laptop. There had to be more to what Ahmadi had told her. She should be able to find it on the internet.

As she opened the laptop and brought up the screen, her cellphone rang.

Intent on the screen, she jumped when it rang beside her. She answered the phone. The caller ID came up as HANDLER.

Kyla's pulse jumped and raced through her veins as she punched the receive button. "Yes, sir."

"Our cover is compromised."

"No shit," she said.

"I've been trying to catch up to you to warn you. You can't trust the agency, and there are others trying to find you."

"Like the ones who sent the drone armed with a missile for me?"

Her handler cursed. "You're getting too close. They don't want their cover blown."

"But they don't mind exposing me," Kyla said. "Who are they?"

"Meet me at Yellowstone Truck Stop in five minutes, and I'll tell you what I know."

"You're in West Yellowstone?"

"Yes. I flew into Bozeman. I was going to a little town called Eagle Rock when I saw that you were on the road headed south."

"Why did you come all this way? Why not tell me what you know over the phone? Why should I trust you? I don't even know what you look like." She regretted that she hadn't insisted on knowing her handler.

"I've been targeted, too," he said. "You need to see

something. Maybe it will help you to figure out what's going on."

"How do I know you're not the one targeting me?"

"You don't. And I don't know if you're the one after me. But I'm taking the chance that you're not one of the bad guys. I'll tell you this, the people who went after you in Kandahar weren't from our organization."

"No? Then who were they? I thought you sent someone to make sure I did the job and then to take me out to clean up the trail."

"I don't work that way."

"Well, that's nice to know," she said. "I still don't trust you."

"Bring your bodyguard. I don't care. Just be there in five. It's not safe for me to be anywhere in one place too long."

"How will I find you?"

"I'll be parked in the back behind the trash bin."

The call ended, and Kyla stared at the phone.

*Five minutes.*

Hell, she didn't have a vehicle. If she was to make it there, she had to borrow one or have someone drive her there.

Kyla flung open her door and ran into Stone's chest.

He caught her and held her until she was steady. "What's wrong?"

"My handler just called. He wants to meet me

at the truck stop. I have to be there in five minutes." She tried to push past him. "I have to go."

Stone caught her arm. "No, you don't. It could be a trap."

"He's in trouble, too. He said I could bring some-one, but it might be better if I go by myself. I don't want you caught in the crossfire."

"You're not going anywhere without me."

"Then come on. We're at four minutes and counting."

"You can get anywhere in town in four minutes," he said as he grabbed her hand and ran down the hallway with her and down the stairs.

They were in the SUV and backing out of the parking lot in one minute.

They made it across town to the truck stop in under five minutes and pulled around to the back of the building.

Kyla pointed. "There's the trash bin."

"I don't see a car."

"Move closer," Kyla urged. She reached into the glove box and pulled out the handgun Stone had stored there.

Stone drove up to the trash bin and edged around it.

A non-descript silver car stood on the other side with the driver's door open.

Kyla's gaze swept the area, searching for people, movement, anything off.

Stone pulled further around the trash bin and car, and they could finally see why the door was open.

A man lay face down on the ground, one foot caught between the body of the car and the door.

"Damn." Kyla flung open her door, jumped down from the SUV and ran to the man on the ground, keeping low and using the open car door as cover

Stone was right behind her, a gun in his hand, pointing at the big trucks parked in the gravel beyond the car.

Kyla knelt beside the man on the ground and touched her fingers to the base of his throat, searching for a pulse.

She didn't find one. Based on the amount of blood, she wasn't surprised. "He was shot."

"He was in the car when he was hit and was either dragged or pulled himself out onto the ground."

Kyla peered into the car. The bullet had gone through the windshield and struck her handler in the chest. "Based on the blood smeared across the passenger seat, he dragged himself."

"Check this out." Stone squatted beside the man pointed toward his hand.

A symbol had been drawn on the pavement in something dark.

"That's blood," Stone clarified. "He drew that in his own blood."

"What is it?" she asked, her focus on the trucks standing in line twenty yards away.

"I'm not sure." Stone pulled out his cellphone and

snapped pictures. "Sending this to Swede." He keyed a message and hit send.

Kyla turned the man's head to get a better look. "Take a picture of his face," she said. "Does Swede have access to facial recognition software and a database?"

"I would assume he does." He took the photo and sent it to Swede as well.

"If he doesn't have access," she said, "I can send it to my contacts." Kyla looked again toward the trucks and glimpsed something moving between a couple of the rigs.

"Get down," she whispered.

Stone dropped to the ground and aimed his handgun toward the trucks.

"They shot him from somewhere in between those parked trucks. Cover me." Holding her gun in front of her, Kyla sprinted across the open space, moving swiftly.

Stone cursed behind her.

When she reached the cab of the first truck, she dropped down on her belly and looked beneath the rigs, searching for shadows or movement. When she didn't see any, she waved for Stone to follow.

He took off running, light on his feet for such a big man.

Kyla saw a shadow move somewhere between the third and fourth truck. She waited until Stone made it safely across the opening, and then moved again. On her hands and knees, she crawled beneath the first trailer, moving as quietly as she could in the gravel, heading for the shadowy figure she'd seen.

After she cleared the trailer of the second truck, she glanced over her shoulder. Stone had low-crawled after her and caught up with her.

She tipped her chin toward the dark figure lying on the ground behind the wheel.

Stone leaned close to her ear and whispered, "I'll swing around the back of the truck and come from behind. Stay put."

She nodded. He'd need time to get into position. In the meantime, she'd keep an eye on him.

Stone moved silently around the back of the truck.

The figure lying behind the wheel shifted.

Kyla tensed. She couldn't let him get away, and Stone wasn't close enough to stop him.

She eased out from under the trailer and had started toward the figure when it disengaged from the shadow and stretched on all four legs.

*Damn.*

The shadow she'd been following was a large, dark dog.

Kyla pushed to her feet and turned toward the end of the truck where Stone had disappeared.

A man rolled out from beneath the trailer and came up in a kneeling position, aiming a rifle in her direction.

Kyla dropped to the ground as a shot rang out. The bullet hit the dirt behind her, kicking up a puff of dust. Kyla tucked her arms against her side and rolled beneath the trailer and out on the other side.

She leaped to her feet and ran the length of the trailer in the direction of the shooter. As she neared the corner, she slowed and eased around. Another shot pierced the metal skin of the trailer above her head. The shooter darted around a red truck cab two trucks over.

Kyla raced toward the first truck and ducked behind it. She dropped to a squat and looked beneath the trailers for movement.

Legs ran the length of the next trailer over.

Kyla ran to catch up. She couldn't let him get away. And she needed to capture him alive.

She wasn't sure where Stone was and couldn't wait for him to find her.

As she neared the end of the trailer, she could hear the sound of feet crunching against gravel, running away. When she reached the end of the long trailer she peered out.

The shooter was running for a car parked near the trees.

Kyla ran out into the open after him.

He looked over his shoulder. When he spotted her, he turned around. While running backward, he loosely aimed at her and pulled the trigger.

The bullets went wide.

Kyla charged forward, undeterred, quickly catching up as the man ripped open the car door, flung his rifle inside and started to get in.

Kyla got to him before he could slide in.

She hit the door with all her momentum, slamming the guy up against the car.

Then she grabbed for his arm and yanked him free of the door.

He staggered, off balance, snagged her arm and fell, taking her down with him.

Kyla landed on her side and immediately rolled away. But not soon enough.

The man flung out his arm and slammed her head against the ground.

Stunned, she lay still, a dark fog blurring her vision. Before it cleared, the man straddled her, pinning her arms to her sides. He cocked his arm.

Kyla flinched in anticipation of the blow.

A blur of movement came at them from the side as Stone threw himself at Kyla's attacker, knocking him off her and into the gravel.

Stone hit him hard enough the man's head bounced against the ground.

When Stone rolled off him, he lay still. Out cold.

Kyla sat up and swayed.

Stone hurried over to her. "Are you okay?"

She nodded, but her head swam. "I am, as long as I don't rock the boat." She looked at the man lying in the gravel. "I'm okay. He's moving. Can't let him get away."

"Stay," Stone said and walked back over to the man lying face-down on the ground and planted his boot on the middle of his back. He pulled his cell-

ELLE JAMES

phone from his pocket. "Yes, I'd like to report a shooting at the truck stop... It was? Great. We have the shooter on the ground. Direct the officer to the area behind where the trucks are parked. Thank you."

Kyla smiled. "Thanks. I thought he was going to rearrange my face, and I kind of like it the way it is."

"Me, too," He smiled across at her.

Moments later, a sheriff's vehicle appeared and came to a stop in the gravel. A deputy climbed out and approached Stone. "Sir, I'll take over from here." He pulled a pair of handcuffs from the clip on his belt and snapped them onto the man's wrists.

"His weapon is in that car," Kyla said.

An ambulance pulled up next, and the emergency medical technicians climbed down and came over to Kyla.

She waved them away and let Stone help her to her feet.

He slipped his arm around her waist.

Kyla leaned into him, glad for his strength, even though her vision had cleared and she felt fine, except for a slight headache.

"You know, you don't have to save the world all by yourself," Stone said.

"I didn't." Her arm circled his waist. "You had my six."

"Barely." He frowned down at her. "We have to work on our timing if we're going to be a team."

Her heart swelled in her chest.

A team. Could it happen? Dare she dream?

# CHAPTER 16

WHEN THEY COULD FINALLY LEAVE the scene, Stone brought the SUV over to Kyla and held the door while she climbed in.

"I wanted to talk to the shooter," Kyla said.

"We all did," Stone frowned. "He wasn't going to say a word without a lawyer." He got behind the wheel and drove back to the lodge, grateful the shooter hadn't hurt Kyla any more than he had.

Bubba, Dax, Moe, Carter and Hunter were just getting into the other SUV when Stone drove up.

They gathered around Stone and Kyla, bombarding them with questions.

"John had his police scanner on when the call came across that there was a shooter at the truck stop," Bubba said. "He went looking for you. When he didn't find you, he got worried and asked us to look into it."

Stone's father burst through the front entrance of the lodge, a frown pulling his eyebrows together in a V. "Stone, thank the Lord. Please tell me you weren't involved in the shooting at the truck stop."

"Okay," Stone said his lips twitching. "I won't tell you."

"We're okay, Mr. Jacobs," Kyla said. "The shooter is in custody."

"Yeah, they said there was one death," His father looked from him to Kyla. "Who was it?"

"My handler." Kyla pressed her fingers to her temple.

"Let's take this inside," Stone said.

Kyla pulled her room key card from her pocket. "Bubba, could you get the laptop from my room and bring it down to the dining room?"

"Absolutely." He took the card and raced up the stairs.

"We can meet in the dining room," John suggested. "They're cleaning up from lunch. You two missed it. Would you like Cookie to make up soup and sandwiches for you?"

"Yes, please," Kyla said.

By the time they'd settled around a large table in the dining room, Bubba was back with the laptop.

Kyla pulled it close and fired it up. She checked her email and found one from Swede. "Look at this."

Swede had sent an image of a logo similar to the rough drawing Kyla's dying handler had drawn on the pavement in his own blood.

Stone read the message aloud for his team to hear. "The logo belongs to Victory Tactical, the controversial mercenaries-for-hire company owned by Ethan Piker."

"I bet they're the same ones who came after me in Kandahar," Kyla said. "But why? And who is paying them?"

Stone's cellphone rang. He pulled it from his pocket and noted Hank's name on the screen. "Hank," he said.

"Bring up the national news," Hank said, "and put me on speaker."

Kyla must have heard him. She brought up the national news channel. One of the headlines showed a picture of Ethan Piker in DC.

Stone hit the speaker button on his cellphone.

"They're accusing Ethan Piker's organization of helping traffic illegal arms sales through Afghanistan to Iraq, using his military for hire teams," Hank said. "They tracked the weapons to a manufacturer in the US. The records show the weapons were sold to the South Korean Army. They never made it to South Korea but showed up in Afghanistan on their way to Iraq. A CIA agent discovered what was going on and reported it to CIA headquarters. The agent has since disappeared."

Kyla exchanged a look with Stone. "Malik."

"They don't mention the agent's name in the article, but Swede did some digging. You're right. It was Agent Malik. In his report, he mentioned the name

Abaddon as the man in charge, and that no one knows who that is.

"We hit a wall trying to trace back through the weapons sales, so we decided to find out who sent Kyla to knock off Ahmadi. I'm not saying how he did it, and I'm sure I don't want to know, but we traced the kill order through your handler, Peter Keller."

"Who is now dead," Stone said.

"It would have been nice to know his name before he died," Kyla muttered.

Hank continued. "Keller received the order to target Ahmadi from a Top-Secret message sent from the office of the National Security Advisor."

"Seriously?" Kyla said.

"Swede traced a recent sizable deposit into Piker's Cayman bank account from a DZK corporation. "We're still digging, but we think we know who it will trace back to. But it's buried deep in a number of corporations."

"Who?" Kyla asked.

"Frank Young," Hank said.

"One of the corporations we found buried in DZK owns a significant number of shares in the weapons manufacturing company supplying the weapons."

"And Frank Young works for the Director of National Intelligence," Stone said. "May I?"

He reached for the laptop and did a search on Frank Young and Ethan Piker. Images popped up of Young with his boss Daniel Mendez. He scrolled past those pictures and came to one of Frank Young at a campaign fundraiser, shaking hands with Ethan Piker. The next image was Frank Young at a different campaign fundraiser, standing with Ethan Piker.

"Finding enough evidence to shut down Young will take time." Hank paused.

"In the meantime, he's got hired killers to take out any loose ends, like me," Kyla said.

"What if he thinks we have the evidence to connect him to the sales?" Stone said. "What if his hometown journalist questions him about his dealings with the weapons manufacturer and threatens to go public?"

Hank chuckled. "You have a journalist in mind? I can get a plane to you in the hour, and Swede can get us on Young's schedule for the morning."

"I'm in," Kyla said.

Stone smiled at Kyla. "I'm her cameraman."

"We need Swede to get us on Young's calendar," Kyla said, her mind already firing.

"Something like a hometown hero interview. We can take it from there."

"You think he'll fall for it?" Hank asked.

"Doesn't hurt to try," Kyla said. "All I know is, until he's caught, I'll have a target on my back. Apparently, he paid Piker to do a job. Piker is persistent."

"Will you be able to get into his office without him or Piker's men recognizing you?" Hank asked.

Kyla smiled. "Absolutely."

Stone had no doubt Kyla would come through. It was his job to make sure Piker's people didn't pick her off before she got there.

# CHAPTER 17

STONE WALKED the hallway like he belonged there, wearing dark slacks, a button-down white shirt and a necktie. He carried a camera case over his shoulder, in character as the cameraman to Ms. Russell's journalist.

"I could get used to you as a blonde," Stone said under his breath. "However, I prefer your dark hair better. It catches the light."

Warmth spread through Kayla.

He leaned closer and whispered, "It reminds me of when the sun glints off my favorite fishing lure."

Kyla snorted, covered her mouth and pretended to cough. She liked that he could tease her while they were on a serious mission inside the offices of the Director of National Intelligence. Swede had worked his magic, and security had issued two visitor's passes and official-looking press badges. He'd also input their fake information in the background database in case any of the security personnel did a formal check between their badges and the database.

The receptionist at the desk had checked Young's schedule to verify their appointment and then waved them through.

They were fifteen minutes early. Young was at a meeting somewhere else. Kyla hoped to distract Young's secretary while Stone slipped into the office and found places to hide the microphones.

Kyla tugged at the short, pastel blue pencil skirt Sadie had sent with Hank in the plane. The flight to DC had taken enough time they'd had to schedule the meeting for late in the afternoon. At first, the secretary hadn't found any openings. When Kyla had explained she was from Mr. Young's hometown and they'd sent her to get an exclusive interview for her hometown heroes column, Young's secretary had found a way to fit them into the schedule.

Kyla entered the office first in her blond wig, blue skirt and white chiffon blouse. Looking good made her feel more confident. Truth was, she'd have felt even more confident in jeans, a soft chambray shirt and boots. The high heels were pretty, but killer.

If all went well and they got what they needed on the voice recorder tucked into the pale blue jacket that matched the skirt, they'd hand over the recording to the DC police and a copy to the Director of National Intelligence.

A detective was on standby with the man who'd killed Peter Keller and had attacked Kyla. When he came to, they'd hit him up for a confession. Once they had that, they'd get a judge to sign off on a warrant for Ethan Piker's arrest.

The secretary glanced up. "Ms. Russell?"

Kyla smiled. "Yes, that's me."

"Have a seat, please. Mr. Young will be back momentarily."

Once Kyla moved away from the secretary's desk, the woman smiled at Stone and batted her eyes. "How can I help you?"

Kyla fought hard to keep from rolling her eyes. Stone couldn't help that he was so darned sexy.

"You wouldn't happen to have a bottle of water, would you?" He gave her a sweet smile that melted every bone in Kyla's body.

"Why yes, of course. Let me get you one." The secretary got up from her desk, went to a small refrigerator built into a credenza and retrieved a small water bottle.

"Thank you," he said and sat across from Kyla, sipping the chilled water.

On cue, the phone on the secretary's desk rang. The woman answered and frowned. "Yes, sir. I can do that. Now?" she asked, looking up at Stone and Kyla. "No, sir. I'll be right there."

As soon as she ended the call, she jumped up, smoothed her skirt and walked calmly toward Kyla and Stone. "Please excuse me for a moment. I have to run a quick errand. Mr. Young will be here any moment. You'll have to introduce yourself. I'm sure he won't mind."

Once they were alone, Stone stood and walked into Frank Young's office. His job was to quickly place the microphones in different locations throughout the room, and then return to the outer office before Young arrived.

Kyla counted the seconds, willing Stone to finish before—

A man walked into the outer office, power-walking through, intent on reaching the inner office uninterrupted.

Kyla's pulse leaped. She stood and hurried to step in front of him. "Mr. Young," she said loud enough for Stone to hear in the other room. With the door slightly open, he would.

Young was forced to stop or run her over.

Kyla pasted a smile on her face and held out her hand. "Mr. Young, I'm Manda Mosley from your hometown of Warrenton, Virginia. I've been sent on a mission to interview you for inclusion in our Hometown Heroes edition of the Warrenton Times. I just need a few minutes of your time. I promise to make it short."

Young glanced at his watch. "This interview is on my calendar?"

She nodded. "Yes, sir."

"Fine." He stepped around her and entered his office. "Well, are you coming?"

Kyla scurried after him, her gaze sweeping the

room for Stone. Besides a massive mahogany desk, a couple of wingback chairs and a long leather sofa, there wasn't much else.

The only place Stone could hide his long body was behind the sofa.

Well, it wasn't quite the way they'd planned, but close. At least Stone was in the room with them.

"You have five minutes," he said, glancing at his watch as he settled in the chair behind his desk. "Go."

Kyla settled across from him in one of the wingback chairs. "I'd like to start with—*What is your connection with DZK industries?*"

Young blinked several times and swallowed hard. "Excuse me?"

"What is your connection to the DZK corporation?"

He leaned forward in his chair. "I don't know what you're talking about."

"Let's try this one." Kyla smiled sweetly. "How much did you pay Ethan Piker to kill the CIA assassin you had sent to Afghanistan to kill Abdul Naser Ahmadi. How much did it cost you to shut him up about the fact you've been shipping arms to Iraq through Afghanistan and using Victory Tactical, Ethan Pike's mercenaries, to make sure they got there?"

She cocked an eyebrow and waited for his response.

He pushed to his feet, his face a ruddy red, his

eyes flashing. "Please leave my office this minute before I call the police."

Kyla stood, her smile gone, her eyes narrowing. "We know who you are and have proof of what you've done. Before the end of today, we'll have Ethan Piker in custody, and with what we have on him, he'll throw you under the bus."

The man pointed to the door. "Out!"

"Not until you answer my questions or confess to the police." She lifted her chin and stood fast. "They're on their way."

"You're insane," he said.

"Maybe. But I'm not the one who's been selling illegal arms to the enemy or putting out kill orders on your own countrymen and women."

"I said get out," he said again.

Kyla persisted. "We have proof of all of this."

"What do you want from me?" he asked. "Are you trying to blackmail me?"

"I could," she said. "We have all the data."

"How much?" he asked.

"How much would it take to keep me quiet?"

His eyes narrowed. "I'm not paying anything. You don't have anything."

"We have one of Piker's men. When he talks, Piker will talk, and your entire operation is going to explode in your face. It's over, Frank."

He charged toward her.

Her heel caught in the carpet, and she fell backward, landing hard on her back.

Young flung himself onto her, straddling her body and trapping her hands. He wrapped his hands around her throat and squeezed. "I know who you are, Kyla Russell. You've caused more than enough trouble. You were supposed to take care of Ahmadi, and then die. You weren't supposed to escape the country, the Taliban and my soldiers. Those shipments will make it to Iraq regardless of your efforts to sabotage me."

Kyla bucked beneath him, her vision beginning to blur.

Then, Stone punched Young in the face and yelled, "Let go of her!"

When Young continued to choke Kyla, Stone put both hands together and swung with all of his might, clipping Young in the side of the head. The man's hands loosed enough for Kyla to roll to one side and out of his reach.

Young staggered to his feet. "You don't have anything on me. It will be my word against yours. I'm going to call the police and have you both arrested for assault.

"We have your confession, Frank. We recorded every word," Stone said.

Kyla rose to her feet. "It's over."

Young kept backing toward his desk until he slipped behind it. "You won't win." He reached into a drawer and pulled out a handgun. "It's not over until I say it's over."

Young pointed the gun at Kyla. "Come any closer,

and I'll shoot her."

Stone walked across the floor, slow and steady. "Give me the gun," he said in a low, insistent tone. "Give yourself up, and they might go easy on your sentence."

Young's eyes rounded. "No. I'm not going to jail. I won't. I can't." He raised the gun, aiming it at Kyla.

Stone stepped between them. "Put the gun down, Frank."

"I can't," he said, his voice shaking. "I can't." Then he pointed the gun toward his own chin, closed his eyes and pulled the trigger.

Kyla held her breath, expecting a loud bang and a bloody mess.

*Click.*

Stone walked forward and took the gun out of the man's hand and then fished in his pocket, pulling out a handful of bullets.

Stone laid the gun on the floor.

Frank Young collapsed in his chair, buried his face in his hands and sobbed.

Seconds later, the Capitol Police burst through the door.

Behind them stood the National Director of Intelligence and Hank Patterson.

Kyla flung herself into Stone's arms and laughed, her laugher catching in her throat on a sob. "I've never been so scared."

He brushed his hand over her hair, holding her close as the police cuffed Young. "You? Scared?"

"Yes, damn it." She leaned back and looked up into his eyes. "I thought he was going to shoot you." A smile spread across her face. "I can't believe you had time to empty his gun."

"It was the first thing I did. I only got one microphone deployed because I took so much time pulling bullets out of the magazine."

"Swede said he got the whole thing on a recording," Hank said as he joined them. "We'll have to answer questions, and they'll want us to stick around a couple of days to sort through what Young was involved in. And the FBI and Department of Homeland Security should be apprehending Ethan Piker as we speak. The man who killed Keller at the truck stop woke up this morning and is talking."

Kyla closed her eyes, drew in a deep breath and let it out. "Thank God."

"I also spoke to my contact in the CIA. The special operations unit wants you back."

Kyla shook her head. "I'm done."

"He said you might say that. They'd take you back into regular operations in a heartbeat. They know your value and don't want to lose a good agent."

Stone took her hand in his. "The other option is to come work with us at Brotherhood Protectors Yellowstone."

Her brow furrowed. "You only hire military men. However, you are in terrible need of additional computer support. Swede is good, but he can't handle it all, not at the rate you're growing."

Stone cocked an eyebrow. "Hank, she has a point."

"Brotherhood Protectors Yellowstone is your baby," Hank said smiling. "You have to man and run it the way you see fit. However, we do need more computer support and someone who can conduct self-defense training. I have a project coming up that she would fit into beautifully."

Stone turned to her. "What's it going to be? Your old job, or something completely different and exciting?"

A grin spread across her face. Maybe there was life after death. "I'm all on board for exciting."

Hank held out his hand.

Kyla took it, and they shook.

"Welcome to the Brotherhood Protectors."

Stone extended his hand to Kyla. She placed hers in his. Instead of shaking it, he pulled her into his arms. "Welcome home, Kyla," he whispered.

Though they stood in the middle of an office building in DC, far from the beauty of Yellowstone, Kyla felt as if she'd come home.

# EPILOGUE

*THREE MONTHS later*

STONE LOOKED around at all they'd accomplished in the past three months and smiled. "Wow. It turned out better than I ever imagined." He pulled Kyla into the circle of his arms. "I couldn't have done it without you."

"And Hank, and Hunter, Bubba, Carter, Dax, Moe, Cookie, Tinker, your father *and* the dozens of skilled craftsmen who pulled this together in such a short amount of time." Kyla wrapped her arms around his middle and leaned her cheek against his chest. "And the best part is that we have living quarters upstairs until we can build our own house."

"Are you sure you don't just want to stay here forever? I mean it has everything, including a gym area with mats to practice your signature move. The guys are still waiting for you to show them how you did that leg clamp."

"Hmm. I'd rather show you." She leaned up on her toes and pressed her lips to his.

He loved when she took her time and explored his mouth with her tongue, and then trailed her lips across his chin and downward.

"I lo—"

Before he completed his sentence, Stone flew through the air and landed flat on his back, the wind knocked from his lungs. Kyla's thighs clamped around his throat, gently, not enough to choke him, but enough to make him hot.

When he could breathe again, he chuckled. "I guess you didn't want to hear what I had to say."

Kyla released her hold around his neck and twisted around to lean over him with a smile. "Me first."

"Okay."

"I heard from Malik and Ahmadi. They're in Texas!" She smiled. "Malik came back to the States and campaigned to get political asylum for Ahmadi and his wife. They all live in Texas in the same neighborhood."

"Did Ahmadi's wife have her baby?"

"She did." Kyla grinned. "A girl."

"That's nice." Stone's brow wrinkled. "Is it my turn now?"

She shook her head. "Let me finish." Kyla touched a finger to her chin and stared around the open interior of the newly renovated interior of the barn. "I think we should've used a lighter shade of gray in here. It's a little dark."

He frowned. "Seriously?"

"Shhh. I'm not done."

"Yes, ma'am."

"We could use a few more chairs around the conference table because we'll be growing and expanding."

"And?" he prompted.

"And we will have a house, and it needs to be in the next eight months because our baby needs a yard to play in, and I want her bedroom to be on the ground floor."

He smiled. "Are you planning on having a baby any time soon? Because I think it's a great idea."

"I was hoping you'd think so because we aren't *planning*, we are *having* a baby in approximately eight months." She reached into her pocket and pulled out a plastic stick. "You know what this means?"

"Are you shitting me?" He sat up, grabbed the stick and stared down at it, his heart racing, his chest so full of emotions he thought he might explode. "We're having a baby!"

Kyla lay back on the mat with a smile spreading across her face. "I never realized how much I wanted this."

He laid on his side next to her and stared down at the joy in her eyes. "A baby?"

She shook her head. "Not just a baby, but *every-*

*thing.*" Kyla cupped his chin. "You, our baby, your father, the Brotherhood...they're all family." She laughed. "I never dreamed how wonderful it could be."

"Only one thing could make it better," he said, staring down at her.

"What? A glass of wine, soaking naked in a hot tub?" She shook her head. "What could make it better than this?"

"If you would be my wife, my partner in crime, my one and only and my everything." He pulled a ring from his pocket and held it out to her. "Kyla, will you marry me?"

Tears welled in her eyes.

"Oh, sweetheart, I didn't mean to make you cry. I love you. If you don't want to marry me, I could be okay as long as you stay with me forever."

She reached up and cupped his cheek. "These are tears of utter joy. Yes. I would be honored to marry you. I want to be with you until we're old and gray and racing our walkers side by side to the end of the hall and back. I love you that much, Stone Jacobs."

"Walkers, huh?" He chuckled. "If that's not true love, I don't know what is."

# ROCKY MOUNTAIN RESCUE

## BROTHERHOOD PROTECTORS
## COLORADO BOOK #2

*New York Times* & *USA Today*
Bestselling Author

# ROCKY MOUNTAIN RESCUE

BROTHERHOOD PROTECTORS

*Colorado*

*New York Times & USA Today* Bestselling Author

# ELLE JAMES

# PROLOGUE

SOMETHING SCRATCHED AT HER LEG.

Then it happened again—pawing, digging, irritating.

She tried to kick her leg to make it stop. However, her legs wouldn't move, and the digging, scratching and pawing continued. When she attempted to move her arms, she couldn't. Her arms and legs would barely budge.

The little effort she expended drained her. Every breath she took weighed heavily on her lungs. Dust filled her nostrils. When she tried to open her eyes, everything was dark. She closed them again. It was too much effort to keep them open. Too much effort to breathe or move. Lying there, she wondered if it would be easier to stop breathing, stop moving and simply go to sleep. Forever.

The scratching stopped. The sound of something sniffing near her ear was followed by more pawing.

This time on the top of her head. Something caught in her hair and pulled.

She tried to turn her head away and tried to raise her arm and slap away whatever was pawing her. A whining sound accompanied the scratching. She didn't want to wake. She wanted to stay asleep, but the persistent pawing made her want to slap away whatever bothered her.

When she tried again to move her arm, this time it shifted just a little. Then it was free. She batted at the thing that punished her head with pawing.

Teeth wrapped around her hand and tugged.

A moan rose up her parched throat. She tried to tell the creature to leave her alone, but her mouth wouldn't open, her eyes wouldn't open. She willed it away, but it persisted.

Darkness faded into light. Warmth permeated her body, chasing away the chill. She moved her head to the side, and dirt shifted off her face exposing it to what felt like sunlight. When she opened her eyes this time the bright glare of sunrise hit her full on. She closed her eyes again.

Teeth sank into her fingers and pulled hard. The whining continued, and a sharp bark sounded in her ear. This time when she opened her eyes, she saw a long snout and a pair of dark eyes staring down at her. The teeth released her hand and the barking continued. The creature latched onto her wrist and pulled, forcing her to roll over. Once lying on her back, she was able to take a deep breath. Again, the animal released her hand and barked and barked and barked.

With each bark, pain radiated through her head. "Please stop. Please," she said. "*Stoooop.*"

It was a dog. The dog ignored her entreaty and continued to bark. Suddenly, it ran away, and silence reigned.

She lay with the sun beating down on her until she couldn't stand it anymore, and she raised her arm to cover her eyes. She must have fallen asleep again.

Voices woke her in a language she didn't understand. Her skin burned in the sunlight. Then a shadow fell over her, and she curled into the fetal position, expecting whoever it was to hit or kick her. Instead, someone draped fabric over her body.

More voices spoke in a language she did not understand. Too tired to open her eyes, she lay still, praying they'd go away. Someone lifted her head and poured water into her mouth. She gulped it thirstily. By the gentle strength in her hands and her soft voice, the person had to be a woman. The others had the same kinds of voices. They were all women. One tried to get her to sit up, but she lay back down, closing her eyes to the harshness of the sun. They left her alone.

After a while—how long, she didn't know—a different voice sounded. Deeper, rougher. "Ma'am?" A hand touched her shoulder.

She whimpered and covered her face with her hand.

The dog was back. Its nose pressed against her cheek, and a long tongue licked the dirt from her face.

"Go on," the voice said.

The dog quit licking her.

"Ma'am, can you hear me? Do you speak English?" the voice asked.

Finally, a language she understood. "Yes," she said, her voice more of a crackling sound than anything else.

"We're going to move you. Ma'am, I'm a medic. Can you tell me your name?"

She blinked her eyes open and looked up into the face of a man.

When the man put his hands on her arms, she tried to fight him, but her arms and legs wouldn't move or work the way they used to.

"No," she said, "*Nooo*." She waved her arms at him, but they did no good. They were too weak to fight.

"It's okay, ma'am. I'm only going to move you," he said, his voice soothing.

"Please," she whispered. "Don't hurt me."

"I'm trying to help you." He looked over his shoulder. "Hey, Johnson, get over here."

"Please, don't hurt me," she murmured, every deep breath shooting pain through her chest.

The man above her turned to somebody else. "Talk to her, Johnson. Maybe it'll help if she has a female to speak to."

A woman wearing an Army desert sand uniform

leaned over her and smoothed the hair back from her forehead. "Hey, I'm Specialist Johnson. We're here to help you. Can you tell me your name?"

She thought and she thought. Name. I have to have a name. I know my name, it's right on the tip of my tongue. What is my name?

"Ma'am, can you tell me your name?" Johnson said.

Tears welled in her eyes and slipped down her cheeks. "I don't...know."

The dog whined, snuck up close to her and pressed his snout to her face.

"Oh, sweetie," Johnson said. "Don't worry. You'll remember. The main thing is to get you somewhere safe so you can heal."

"Come on," the man said. "Let's get her on the stretcher and into the chopper."

Men lifted her and laid her on a stretcher. She fought until they strapped her down. The dog tried to jump on the stretcher with her.

"It must be hers. Take it with you," a man said.

The woman named Johnson scooped the dog up into her arms and carried it with her as they loaded her onto the helicopter.

Then someone stuck a needle into her arm. Sunlight dimmed and darkness overtook her. As consciousness faded to black, her name came to her, and she whispered, "JoJo."

# ABOUT THE AUTHOR

ELLE JAMES also writing as MYLA JACKSON is a *New York Times* and *USA Today* Bestselling author of books including cowboys, intrigues and paranormal adventures that keep her readers on the edges of their seats. When she's not at her computer, she's traveling, snow skiing, boating, or riding her ATV, dreaming up new stories. Learn more about Elle James at www.ellejames.com

Website | Facebook | Twitter | GoodReads | Newsletter | BookBub | Amazon

Or visit her alter ego Myla Jackson at mylajackson.com
Website | Facebook | Twitter | Newsletter

*Follow Me!*
www.ellejames.com
ellejamesauthor@gmail.com

# ALSO BY ELLE JAMES

Shadow Assassin

### *Delta Force Strong*

Ivy's Delta (Delta Force 3 Crossover)

Breaking Silence (#1)

Breaking Rules (#2)

Breaking Away (#3)

Breaking Free (#4)

Breaking Hearts (#5)

Breaking Ties (#6)

Breaking Point (#7)

Breaking Dawn (#8)

Breaking Promises (#9)

### *Brotherhood Protectors Yellowstone*

Saving Kyla (#1)

Saving Chelsea (#2)

Saving Amanda (#3)

Saving Liliana (#4)

Saving Breely (#5)

Saving Savvie (#6)

Saving Jenna (#7)

Full Force (#3)

Driving Force (#4)

Tactical Force (#5)

Disruptive Force (#6)

### *Mission: Six*

One Intrepid SEAL

Two Dauntless Hearts

Three Courageous Words

Four Relentless Days

Five Ways to Surrender

Six Minutes to Midnight

### *Hearts & Heroes Series*

Wyatt's War (#1)

Mack's Witness (#2)

Ronin's Return (#3)

Sam's Surrender (#4)

### *Take No Prisoners Series*

SEAL's Honor (#1)

SEAL'S Desire (#2)

SEAL's Embrace (#3)

SEAL's Obsession (#4)

SEAL's Proposal (#5)

SEAL's Seduction (#6)

Hot Velocity (#4)

## *Cajun Magic Mystery Series*

Voodoo on the Bayou (#1)

Voodoo for Two (#2)

Deja Voodoo (#3)

Cajun Magic Mysteries Books 1-3

## *SEAL Of My Own*

Navy SEAL Survival

Navy SEAL Captive

Navy SEAL To Die For

Navy SEAL Six Pack

## *Devil's Shroud Series*

Deadly Reckoning (#1)

Deadly Engagement (#2)

Deadly Liaisons (#3)

Deadly Allure (#4)

Deadly Obsession (#5)

Deadly Fall (#6)

## *Covert Cowboys Inc Series*

Triggered (#1)

Taking Aim (#2)

Bodyguard Under Fire (#3)

Cowboy Resurrected (#4)

Navy SEAL Justice (#5)

Navy SEAL Newlywed (#6)

High Country Hideout (#7)

Clandestine Christmas (#8)

*Thunder Horse Series*

Hostage to Thunder Horse (#1)

Thunder Horse Heritage (#2)

Thunder Horse Redemption (#3)

Christmas at Thunder Horse Ranch (#4)

*Demon Series*

Hot Demon Nights (#1)

Demon's Embrace (#2)

Tempting the Demon (#3)

*Lords of the Underworld*

Witch's Initiation (#1)

Witch's Seduction (#2)

The Witch's Desire (#3)

Possessing the Witch (#4)

*Stealth Operations Specialists (SOS)*

Nick of Time

Alaskan Fantasy

*Boys Behaving Badly Anthologies*

Rogues (#1)

Blue Collar (#2)

Pirates (#3)

Stranded (#4)

First Responder (#5)

Blown Away

Warrior's Conquest

Enslaved by the Viking Short Story

Conquests

Smokin' Hot Firemen

Protecting the Colton Bride

Protecting the Colton Bride & Colton's Cowboy Code

Heir to Murder

Secret Service Rescue

High Octane Heroes

Haunted

Engaged with the Boss

Cowboy Brigade

Time Raiders: The Whisper

Bundle of Trouble

Killer Body

Operation XOXO

An Unexpected Clue

Baby Bling

Under Suspicion, With Child

Texas-Size Secrets

Cowboy Sanctuary

Lakota Baby

Dakota Meltdown

Beneath the Texas Moon

Made in the USA
Monee, IL
22 August 2023

41461412R00144